This book
belongs to

_____

BRADY BRADY

All-Star Hockey Collection

BRADY BRADY

All-Star Hockey Collection

Written by **Mary Shaw**
Illustrated by **Chuck Temple**

Scholastic Canada Ltd.
Toronto New York London Auckland Sydney
Mexico City New Delhi Hong Kong Buenos Aires

Scholastic Canada Ltd.
604 King Street West, Toronto, Ontario M5V 1E1, Canada

Scholastic Inc.
557 Broadway, New York, NY 10012, USA

Scholastic Australia Pty Limited
PO Box 579, Gosford, NSW 2250, Australia

Scholastic New Zealand Limited
Private Bag 94407, Botany, Manukau 2163, New Zealand

Scholastic Children's Books
Euston House, 24 Eversholt Street, London NW1 1DB, UK

www.scholastic.ca

Library and Archives Canada Cataloguing in Publication
Shaw, Mary, 1965-
[Novels. Selections]
Brady Brady all-star hockey collection / Mary Shaw ; illustrated by
Chuck Temple.

Contents: Brady Brady and the great exchange -- Brady Brady and the
great rink -- Brady Brady and the most important game -- Brady Brady
and the puck on the pond -- Brady Brady and the runaway goalie.
ISBN 978-1-4431-2845-2 (bound)

1. Children's stories, Canadian. I. Temple, Chuck, 1962-, illustrator
II. Shaw, Mary, 1965- . Brady Brady and the great exchange. III. Title.

PS8587.H3473A6 2013   jC813'.6   C2013-903008-5

6 5 4 3 2 1   Printed in China 38   13 14 15 16 17

Contents

BRADY BRADY

and the Great Rink

Brady loved winter. He loved winter because he loved to skate.
He loved to skate because he loved hockey.
Hockey was all Brady thought about.

It drove his family **crrrazy**!
They had to call him twice
to get his attention.

"Brady, Brady!
Stop thinking about hockey.
Eat your potatoes."

"Brady, Brady! Brush your teeth."

"Brady, Brady! Get ready for school."

"Brady, Brady! Don't forget your lunch."

Everyone got so used to calling him twice that they simply named him Brady Brady.

It was easier that way.

7

Brady was on a team called the Icehogs.
When hockey season arrived and the Icehogs started to play,
Brady thought less about everything else
and even more about hockey.

When Brady wasn't playing hockey, he was "snow-watching." Every morning he leapt out of bed to see if a storm had dumped snow in his backyard. Back in the summer he had decided that when the snow came, he would build something incredible! One Saturday morning it finally happened. The backyard was covered in snow.

"Whoo-hoo!" he shouted, shaking the dog's basket. "Come on, Hatrick! We've got work to do."

"Slow down, pal," his dad chuckled, as Brady gobbled down his cereal. "Where's the fire?"

"No fire, Dad. Just snow. Lots of it!" Climbing up onto his chair, Brady announced, "Today I am going to build the greatest backyard rink ever! Kids will come from all over town to play hockey on it."

"You're crazy. It's too much work," said his sister.

"Brady Brady, your nose will freeze off," warned his mom.

"I'd help, but I'm allergic to the cold," muttered his dad.

"That's OK. I can do it myself," Brady boasted as he bundled up in his snowsuit, boots, and hat. His mom helped with the mittens — two pairs, to stay extra warm.

Brady shuffled his feet in the snow
and made the outline of his rink.
It was as big as the whole backyard.

With his dad's big shovel,
Brady heaved snow
over to the sides.

Snowbanks grew higher and higher, but not quite high
enough to block the sight of his sister drinking hot chocolate
in the warm kitchen.

Brady could hardly lift the sandwich his mother brought out
for lunch. As he pounded down the snow to make
his rink smooth, Brady was certain it was
his arms — not his nose — that would fall off.

It was almost dark when Brady finished his pounding.
He took a squirt bottle full of raspberry juice and drew a
red face-off circle. With a squirt bottle of blueberry juice he
drew two blue lines, just like on a real hockey rink. He dragged
the hose out and began flooding his rink. The water froze.
Brady almost froze along with it.

That night he collapsed into bed, barely able to move.
"See, Mom?" he sniffed. "My nose didn't fall off."

In the morning, Brady woke up to find his rink buried in snow.

"I told you it was too much work," said his sister.

"Brady Brady, you'll turn into a snowman," warned his mom.

"Too bad I have such a bad back," muttered his dad.

After shoveling for hours, Brady flooded his rink. When Hatrick chased a squirrel across it, he flooded the rink once more.

Again, he fell into bed at night, barely able to give his mom a hug.

On snowy days Brady shoveled his rink.

On really cold days he flooded his rink.

And every day, no matter how
tired or cold he was,
Brady skated on his rink.

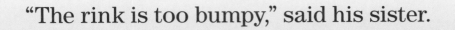

"The rink is too bumpy," said his sister.

"You'll wear yourself out," warned his mom.

"I can't find my skates," muttered his dad.

21

Brady would skate for hours.
He practiced his crossovers, backwards skating, and stopping.
Sometimes Hatrick helped by standing in net
while Brady perfected his shot.

Brady's skating got better and better.
And just in time. Tomorrow the Icehogs
were playing in their biggest game yet — the Frosty Cup.

That night Brady was so excited, he slept in his equipment.

Brady was the first to arrive in the dressing room.
He high-fived his teammates as they came in,
hoping they were as pumped up about the game as he was.

When everyone had their uniforms on and skates laced up,
they huddled in the center of the room and began their team cheer.

"We've got the power,
We've got the might,
We've got the spirit . . .

They waited and waited. Finally the coach spoke up. "Looks like the power is out in the whole building. I'm afraid we can't play for the Frosty Cup after all. Everyone take off your equipment."

Brady didn't need any lights on to know what his teammates looked like. He could hear the moans and groans as they started to unlace their skates in the dark. They were as heartbroken as he was.

"Wait!" cried Brady. "I know a *great* rink where we can play."

29

It was the coolest hockey game ever played.
People came from all over town.

It was so much fun that nobody even cared about the score!

And when Brady saw the happy faces around him, he knew he truly had built the greatest backyard rink *ever*!

BRADY BRADY

and the Runaway Goalie

Brady loved winter. He loved winter because he loved hockey.
Hockey was all he thought about. He thought about it so much
that everyone had to call him twice to get his attention.
It drove his family *crrrazy*!

"Brady, Brady! Is your bed made?"

"Brady, Brady! Hatrick wants out."

"Brady, Brady! You're spilling your milk!"

Pretty soon they just called him Brady Brady. It was easier that way.

Brady was on a team called the Icehogs.
The rink they played at was right around the
corner from Brady's house. It wasn't far, but Brady
always left early so he could be the first one there.

One Saturday morning, the Icehogs were playing a nasty
team called the Dragoons. The Dragoons were **undefeated.**
Brady was excited and a little nervous as he headed to the rink.

On the way in, Brady always said hello to his friend, Chester.
Chester was the Icehogs' goalie, and the smartest kid Brady knew.
He often helped Brady with his math.

Chester also helped at the concession stand before every game.
He said munching on popcorn, instead of thinking about flying pucks,
got rid of the butterflies in his stomach.

Brady noticed that Chester looked especially jittery today.
"See you in the dressing room, Chester." Brady waved on his way past.

"Sure, Brady Brady," mumbled Chester, but he did not wave back.

There was usually a lot of chatter before a game,
but today the Icehogs' dressing room was almost silent.
The Dragoons' nasty reputation had the Icehogs worried.

When everyone was dressed, they gathered in the center
of the room for their team cheer. It wasn't quite as loud as usual.

"We've got the power,
We've got the might,
We've got the spirit . . .

. . . Something isn't right!"

They looked around the room . . . and saw a heap of goalie equipment.

Chester was missing!

"Brady Brady! See if you can find him," said the Coach.
Brady rushed away as fast as he could. A second later he was back
holding a note that had been taped to the door.

Brady read it out loud.

"Oh, no!" groaned the Coach. "We can't play without our goalie!"

Some of the kids sat down and began to unlace their skates.
"Wait!" cried Brady. "We *do* have a goalie.
We just have to *find* him."

They checked behind
the popcorn machine at the
concession stand.
No Chester.

They checked under the bleachers.
There were blobs of gum stuck
to the bottom of the seats,
but no Chester.

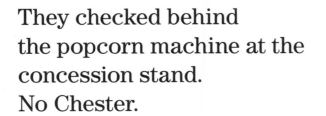

48

They checked everywhere — even the girls' washroom.

No Chester.

Finally, they checked the Zamboni garage. There was Chester, on top of the ice machine.

"Come down, Chester. We need you," Brady pleaded with his friend.

"I just can't face the Dragoons, Brady Brady," Chester whimpered. "I'm scared."

"You don't have to face them alone, son," said the Coach. "We're the Icehogs. We stick together."

"We're all a bit nervous, Chester," Brady added. "But you can outsmart the Dragoons any day."

The rest of the Icehogs started to cheer. This time they were as loud and as proud as ever.

> *"We've got the power,*
> *We've got the might,*
> *Chester's our goalie,*
> *He's all right!"*

Chester climbed down from the Zamboni.

51

Out on the rink, the Icehogs lined up against the Dragoons. Brady could hear Chester's teeth chattering behind his mask. The ref dropped the puck and the game began.

The Dragoons tripped and slashed and played a pretty mean game, but the Icehogs didn't give up. They knew they had to play hard and help Chester out — especially since he had his eyes shut most of the time.

When the final buzzer sounded, there was no score.
In overtime no one scored. That meant only one thing . . .
a sudden death shoot-out!

Chester tried to leave the ice, but his teammates dragged him back.

"Come on, Chester, you can do it," Brady said, patting his friend on the back. "You can do anything you put your mind to."

The Icehogs were to go first,
and Brady was picked to shoot.
Starting at center ice, he raced toward
the goalie with the puck on the end of his stick.
He could hear the cheers of his teammates.

Brady fired the puck.
There was a *ping* as it nicked the crossbar — and flew into the net!
The crowd went wild, except for the Dragoons' fans, of course.

57

It was the Dragoons' turn to shoot. Brady looked at Chester and gave him a thumbs-up. "Remember, Chester, you can do anything you put your mind to!"

The Dragoons player began his charge. Sweat trickled down Chester's face, but he didn't close his eyes. Instead, he began to think.

"The speed of the puck . . . times the arc of the puck . . ."
Chester muttered, ". . . that means it should land . . . *riiight* . . .

. . . HERE!"

Thwack!
The puck landed in
Chester's outstretched glove.

"Holy moly! What a goalie!" the Icehogs hollered.
They jumped over the boards to mob Chester,
who still hadn't moved.

61

Chester was still holding the game puck as they hoisted him onto their shoulders.

"I knew you could do it!" Brady said proudly to his friend. His friend — and the Icehogs' *great* goalie.

BRADY BRADY
and the Great Exchange

It was game day and the Icehogs huddled in the center of the dressing room for their team cheer.

"*We've got the power,*
We've got the might,
They call us the Icehogs,
And we're outta sight!"

Then, one by one, they filed out the door giggling. Everybody but Gregory.

At the start of the hockey season, Gregory had told his teammates that he needed a few minutes alone to focus on his game. He always remained in the dressing room while the others took to the ice to warm up. So, the Icehogs left Gregory alone. After all, they had their superstitions, too.

Brady **always** had to be the first one at the rink.

Chester would **not** play without munching on popcorn first.

Tes made her dad take the exact same route to the rink every time — avoiding all potholes and sewers.

Tree would hum as he put on his equipment — first the left side, and then the right.

When the warm-up began, Brady realized he had forgotten the water bottles and returned to the dressing room to get them. There was Gregory, cheeks puffed out, sweat rolling down his forehead, as he fought to wedge his feet into his skates.

"Are you okay, Gregory?" Brady asked his red-faced teammate.

"I . . . I'm fine, Brady Brady," answered Gregory, as he quickly wiped a sweat ball off his nose. "I'll be right out." Brady picked up the water bottles and turned to leave.

He knew his friend wasn't telling the truth. "If you don't feel well," Brady said, "maybe you shouldn't play today."

71

Gregory looked sadly at his friend. "I don't want to let the team down, but I can't go out there today . . . or any other day."

"What are you talking about?" Brady asked.

In barely a whisper, Gregory leaned over to Brady and said sadly, "My skates don't fit me anymore and my parents can't buy me new ones right now. It hurts to skate."

As Gregory began to pack up his equipment bag, Brady noticed his red, puffy feet. Gregory had stopped wearing his tie-dyed socks a month ago. His teammates had found this strange because Gregory had always claimed that the thick, green socks were his good luck charm. Now Brady knew what was wrong.

Brady rifled through his
equipment bag and pulled out
a bottle of lotion.

"My mom put this in my bag 'cause she says my gloves give me
stinky hands. If we rub some lotion on your feet, maybe they'll
slide right into your skates!" Brady suggested. "Do you think
you could just play once more in these? Then later we can figure
out what to do."

This made Gregory **and** his feet feel much better.

Gregory tried not to think about the pain in his toes as he skated up and down the ice. But by the third period, Brady could see that his friend was hurting. He suggested that Gregory just stand in front of the net, so that Brady could pass the puck to him as much as possible.

Nobody seemed to notice anything was wrong, and both boys were relieved when the final buzzer sounded.

The Icehogs' dressing room was filled with
the usual post-game chatter.

It was Chester who gave Brady the great idea.

"I think I'd like to play with bigger arm pads," Chester said as he flexed his scrawny muscles. "I bet it would help me take up more room in the net."

"My mom would love it if I got rid of these smelly gloves," Brady chimed in. "So, I've got a *great* idea!"

Everyone stopped and listened.

"We'll have the biggest equipment exchange ever! Bring anything you can't wear anymore, and maybe you can swap it for something else!" Brady said, winking at Gregory.

The Icehogs loved the idea.

They spent the rest of the day putting up flyers around town,
announcing the **_great_** hockey exchange at Brady's **_great_** backyard rink.

Brady and Gregory were so excited,
they both had trouble sleeping.

When the big day arrived, Gregory was the first one to show up, his too-small skates tucked under his arm. Brady had made signs that poked up from the snowbanks at each corner of the rink.

Gregory placed his skates under the "SKATES" sign.
People arrived from all over town.

Brady spotted the perfect pair of gloves. He was sure that they would help him score some big goals.

Chester found a big set of arm pads. He was certain nobody would be able to get anything past him.

Gregory sat patiently waiting for skates his size — the excitement on his face fading each time he checked a pair of skates that were placed under the "SKATES" sign.

All were either way too small, or way too big.

Gregory was about to give up hope when Brady walked out of his house and over to the pile, placing his own skates under the sign.

"What are you doing, Brady Brady?" Gregory asked as he picked them up. "You skate like the wind in these!"

Brady nodded. "It's time for someone else to skate like the wind in them."

Gregory's feet slid right in. "PERFECT!" they both shouted.

Gregory raced off to test out his new skates. Brady stared at the pile in front of him. None of the skates were his size. Finally, he settled for a pair and tried them on.

As Brady laced them up, Gregory skated back and pulled something out of his pocket.

"Those look a bit big, Brady Brady. Here, try these on for size," he said, proudly holding up his green, tie-dyed socks. "They'll help your skates fit and bring you good luck."

Gregory was right. The lucky socks did make Brady's feet fit better in the skates.

The streetlights were coming on as the last happy customers left the backyard. Brady and Gregory had the whole rink to themselves. The only equipment that nobody had wanted . . .

. . . was Brady's smelly gloves.

BRADY BRADY
and the Most Important Game

Brady had been taking shots on Chester all morning.
When Chester needed a break, Hatrick took his spot in net.
Brady and his friend were determined to practice. This weekend
they would play in the biggest hockey tournament of the season,
The Gold Stick.
Not only was it the biggest tournament of the season, it was being
played at the Icehogs' home rink.
The Icehog players put up posters all over town to let everyone
know about the important weekend.

Brady had been counting the days until the big weekend arrived. The night before the tournament, Brady was so excited, he slept in his equipment.

He dreamt about racing up the ice on a breakaway, sparks flying from his skates, and scoring the tournament-winning goal.

When Brady yelled "HE SCORES!!!" in his sleep, Hatrick jumped right out of his basket.

97

Brady high-fived his teammates as they arrived in the dressing room. All the Icehogs agreed that tournaments were the best part of playing hockey. Everyone was excited about meeting other players and trading team pins at center ice.

The stands were packed with parents, grandparents, brothers, sisters, and players from other teams.

When Tree sang the anthem at the opening game,
the crowd went wild!

The Icehogs battled hard every game and their efforts paid off.
The next day, they would be playing for *The Gold Stick.*

"Make sure you eat a healthy dinner and get a good night's sleep,"
their coach told them.

"Oh, and Brady Brady, don't forget to dry out your smelly hockey gloves," he said with a wink.

Brady slept in his equipment again that night.

103

On the morning of their most important game, the Icehogs arrived early to find out who they would be playing against. A loud groan could be heard throughout the rink as the coach announced . . . "Team, we're playing the DRAGOONS!"

The Dragoons loved to wait until the referee had his back turned, and then see how many Icehogs they could trip.

Tes bit her bottom lip. Tree hummed nervously. Brady tied Chester's skates together so that he couldn't run away.

When everyone was dressed, they gathered in the center of the room for their team cheer.

"We've got the power,
We've got the might,
Hey Dragoons,
Kiss The Gold Stick good night!"

Out on the rink, the Icehogs lined up against the Dragoons.

The ref dropped the puck and the game began. The Dragoons tripped and slashed, and played a pretty mean game, but the Icehogs did not give up.

The Dragoons' coach played his best player most of the game.
Some Dragoons did not get to play at all.

The Icehogs' coach told his players, "We made it here as a team, and everyone on the team will play."

The game was tied as the third period began, and the Icehogs were bruised and battered.

The Dragoons had been spraying snow in Chester's mask all game.

Tes had been body checked while doing her Twirlin' Torpedo,

and Gregory was
slashed on a breakaway.

NEVER in his life
had Brady wanted to
win a game so badly.

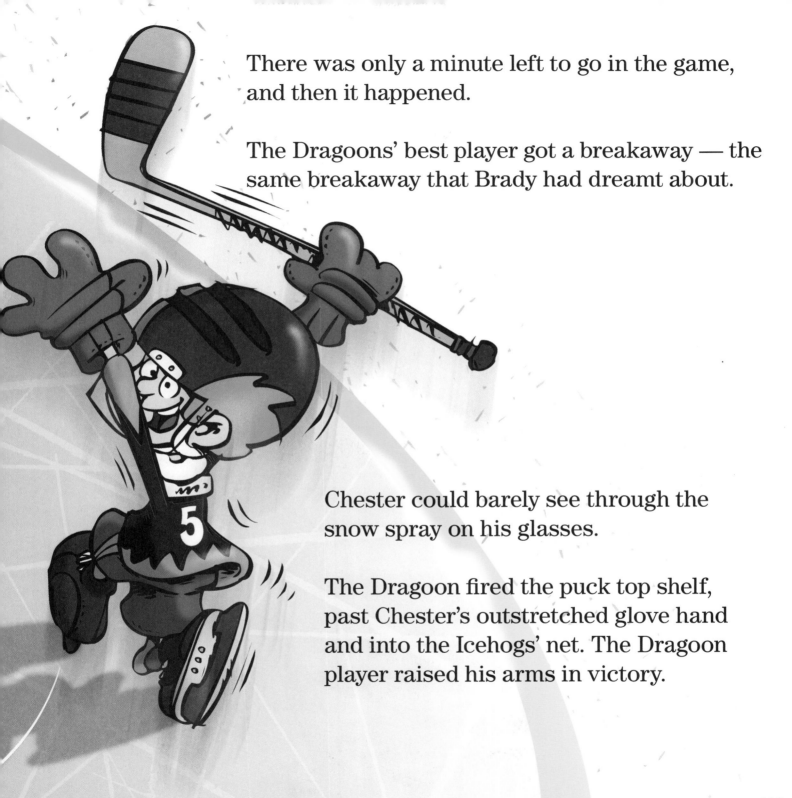

There was only a minute left to go in the game, and then it happened.

The Dragoons' best player got a breakaway — the same breakaway that Brady had dreamt about.

Chester could barely see through the snow spray on his glasses.

The Dragoon fired the puck top shelf, past Chester's outstretched glove hand and into the Icehogs' net. The Dragoon player raised his arms in victory.

Brady could see the Dragoons fans in the stands whistling and screaming at the top of their lungs. The Icehogs fans were leaving the stands. Brady's dad gave him a weak smile as he walked past the glass.

The final seconds of the game seemed to last forever. Finally, the buzzer sounded. The game was over. The Icehogs had lost *The Gold Stick.*

Reluctantly, the team lined up to shake hands with the Dragoons, and then skated off the ice with their heads lowered.

The dressing room was silent. Tears rolled down several of the Icehogs' faces. Chester buried his head between his pads.

Brady didn't like to lose. Losing made his heart feel heavy.

Coach walked to the center of the room with a HUGE smile on his face. "Icehogs, I know it's hard right now, but try to remember how hard you worked to get to this final game. And if you only learn one thing in your hockey lives, remember this: it's more important to lose fairly than to win by cheating."

The Icehogs began to take off their equipment. Suddenly, there was a loud knock on the dressing room door. Brady peeked his head out.

"WAIT! Everyone keep your equipment on!" Brady yelled to his friends. "That wasn't our most important game. The NEXT one is!"

When Brady flung open the door,
the Icehogs collapsed with laughter when they saw who would
meet them on the ice.

Brady didn't know who was more excited
about the most important game —
the Icehogs or their parents.
But he did know that his heart
didn't feel heavy anymore.

BRADY BRADY

and the Puck on the Pond

Brady loved winter. He loved winter because he loved to skate. Brady would skate on his backyard rink every chance he got.

One afternoon, Brady and a few of his friends were playing a game of shinny when Freddie, one of Brady's teammates on the Icehogs, came rushing into the backyard.

"Brady Brady! You should see the **size** of the hockey rink on my grandpa's pond!" said Freddie excitedly. "It's the biggest and best rink **ever**! You guys should come over and play!"

"That sounds awesome!" Tes squealed.

"I can't wait!" Kev added.

"Let's go put the puck on the pond!" Chester hollered.

Brady watched his friends as they rushed off the ice to follow Freddie. This was the first time that his friends wanted to play shinny somewhere else. Brady gripped his hockey stick tightly, and tried not to show how sad he felt.

"You guys go ahead and have fun. I have to stay and help my dad with some chores," Brady lied. "Maybe I'll catch up with you later."

As the kids gathered at the pond, Freddie's grandpa high-fived them and showed them the cool benches he had made out of snow. Freddie was quick to point out the blue lines and red circle in the middle of the ice.

"See?" said Freddie.
"Just like Brady
Brady's rink!"

The Icehogs were having way too much fun on Freddie's rink to miss Brady. They thought it was cool to play on such a big rink. When they took turns sitting on the bench, Freddie's grandpa brought them cups of hot chocolate filled with colored marshmallows.

"This is the **best** rink ever!" said Tes between sips of hot chocolate.

The next morning, Brady wolfed down his breakfast, grabbed his stick, and headed out to his backyard rink. He wanted to have his rink all shoveled off and ready for the Icehogs — but Brady's friends had something else in mind.

"Hey, Brady Brady," said Tree, "we're going over to Freddie's pond. Do you want us to wait while you get your skates?"

"No, you go ahead. I have to help my dad again," said Brady with a frown. "I'll catch up with you guys later." But Brady knew he wouldn't be catching up with them later.

He put on his skates and practiced his slapshot with his dog, Hatrick. It wasn't as much fun as it usually was. Even Hatrick got bored and walked off the ice with the puck between his teeth.

That night at dinner, Brady didn't have much of an appetite.

"What's wrong, Brady Brady?" asked his mother.

"Yeah, you don't seem like yourself lately," said his father. "You've been moping around the house for the last couple of days."

137

Brady took a deep breath and let out a big sigh. "All of my friends want to play with Freddie instead of me," he explained. "His grandpa has a big ice rink on his pond, with benches made out of snow. The kids don't want to play on my rink anymore. I **won't** play on Freddie's pond — even if it means that I have to stop playing with my friends!"

"You could do that, Brady Brady, but don't you think you would be lonely?" his mother asked.

"There's only room for one rink in this neighborhood!" muttered Brady.

The next day, Brady's friends were waiting at the end of his driveway once again. This time Brady convinced them that they should have a game of shinny on **his** rink.

"It's too far to carry all of our equipment to the pond. Anyway . . . I hear that Freddie doesn't even have any nets," said Brady. "Who's heard of using boots for goalie nets?"

The Icehogs didn't care; they just wanted somewhere to play.

As Freddie shoveled the pond, he wondered
why the Icehogs had not arrived. He thought everyone
was going to meet at the pond first thing in the morning.
After all, his friends seemed to like playing hockey on his
grandpa's pond.

Freddie finished cleaning off the rink, but there was still no
sign of his teammates. He decided to try and find out what his
friends were doing.

As he walked through the neighborhood, he could hear laughter coming from Brady's backyard.

"Hey," said Freddie. "I was waiting for everyone to come and play a game on the pond. What happened?"

"Everyone decided to play on my rink instead," Brady boasted. "Plus, you don't have any hockey nets, so how do you expect us to have a **real** game?"

Freddie turned and left Brady's backyard with his head hung low. "That wasn't a very nice thing to say to Freddie," whispered Chester. "He's your friend."

Suddenly, Brady didn't feel like playing anymore. He remembered how sad he felt when he had no one to play with. Determined to make things right, Brady knew that he needed to come up with a plan.

"Wait!" cried Brady. "I have a great idea! Why don't we meet early tomorrow morning, and we'll surprise Freddie by cleaning off his grandpa's pond! I'm sure he could use a few friends to help him out!" The kids all nodded in agreement.

"I have a couple of old hockey nets that would be perfect for the pond. We can bring them in the morning," said Brady.

Brady got up early the next morning. He grabbed his skates, his stick, and his dad's big shovel. His friends were already waiting on his driveway. They gathered up the extra hockey nets and whisked them off to the pond.

"We've got some work to do," said Brady, as he heaved snow over
to the side of the frozen pond. Everyone pitched in to help.
They even made snowmen to be the "fans in the stands."

When Freddie arrived at the pond, he could not believe his eyes. The ice had been completely shoveled and the old winter boots had been replaced by Brady's hockey nets.

"Hey!" yelled Brady, as Freddie walked over to the benches. "How about a game of shinny?"

As Freddie's face lit up, Brady realized that it was his friends . . . *not* the rink . . . that made the game fun!

LIBBY WIMBLEY

ROOSTER INSTRUCTOR

by Amy Cobb illustrated by Alexandria Neonakis

Calico Kid

An Imprint of Magic Wagon
abdopublishing.com

For Mara. Always believe in yourself. With special appreciation to Heidi for your kindness and encouragement. –AC

For John, Gooby and Kitty, whose love and support make my career possible. –AN

abdopublishing.com

Published by Magic Wagon, a division of ABDO, PO Box 398166, Minneapolis, Minnesota 55439. Copyright © 2018 by Abdo Consulting Group, Inc. International copyrights reserved in all countries. No part of this book may be reproduced in any form without written permission from the publisher. Calico Kid™ is a trademark and logo of Magic Wagon.

Printed in the United States of America, North Mankato, Minnesota.
052017
092017

THIS BOOK CONTAINS RECYCLED MATERIALS

Written by Amy Cobb
Illustrated by Alexandria Neonakis
Edited by Heidi M.D. Elston
Art Directed by Laura Mitchell

Publisher's Cataloging-in-Publication Data

Names: Cobb, Amy, author. | Neonakis, Alexandria, illustrator.
Title: Rooster instructor / by Amy Cobb ; illustrated by Alexandria Neonakis.
Description: Minneapolis, MN : Magic Wagon, 2018. | Series: Libby Wimbley
Summary: Libby's rooster, Doodle, doesn't crow. He peeps. So, Libby starts
    Rooster School just for Doodle. She tries everything to teach him how to crow,
    but he just says peep. In a huff, she cancels Rooster School. A few days later
    while catching frogs, Libby hears Doodle crow from the barn!
Identifiers: LCCN 2017930831 | ISBN 9781532130267 (lib. bdg.) |
    ISBN 9781614798538 (ebook) | ISBN 9781614798583 (Read-to-me ebook)
Subjects: LCSH: Roosters–Juvenile fiction. | School–Juvenile fiction. |
    Friendship–Juvenile fiction.
Classification: DDC [Fic]–dc23
LC record available at http://lccn.loc.gov/2017930831

Table of Contents

Chapter 1

Doodle Trouble

Libby Wimbley lived on a farm.
She lived with her mom and dad
and little brother, Stewart.

In the barn lived three goats, two
cows, a pony, some hens, and one
rooster named Doodle.

There was only one problem: Each morning, Libby listened. But Doodle never crowed!

On Sunday morning, he roosted.

On Monday morning, he pecked ants.

On Tuesday morning, he chased the hens.

On Wednesday morning, he snoozed.

On Thursday morning, he flapped his wings.

On Friday morning, he scratched in the dirt.

And on Saturday morning, he stayed in the chicken coop until after noon.

"Why doesn't Doodle crow every morning like a normal rooster?" Libby finally asked Dad.

"Doodle's still a young chick," Dad said. "He doesn't know how."

"This summer, I'll teach him," Libby said.

Mom looked surprised. "You'll teach Doodle to crow?"

Libby smiled proudly. "That's right. Doodle's going to school. Rooster School!"

"When?" asked Stewart.

"First thing in the morning," Libby said.

Chapter 2

Rooster School

The next day, Libby woke up extra early. She raced to the barn.

"Good morning, everyone," Libby said to all of the animals in her best teacher voice. "It's the first day of Rooster School."

Elvis, the goat, bleated softly.

"Don't worry, Elvis," Libby said.
"Goats don't go to Rooster School.
Go back to chewing your cud."

And Elvis did.

"So who does go to Rooster
School?" Libby asked.

If the animals knew, they didn't
answer.

"Well," Libby went on, "Rooster School students have feathers. And a beak. And funny little chicken legs."

Libby looked at Doodle. "Does that student sound like anyone you know, Doodle?"

Doodle fluffed his feathers. *Peep*!?

"No, not peep!" Libby said.
"Roosters crow, like this. Cock-a-doodle-do!"

Doodle cocked his head to one side.

"That's it, Doodle!" Libby said, hopefully.

But all Doodle said was, *Peep*!?

"Repeat after me, Doodle," Libby said. "Cock-a-doodle-do!"

Peep! said Doodle.

Libby even showed Doodle a picture of a rooster. "See? Right here it says C-R-O-W."

C-R-O-W

Doodle pecked at the paper bird. But he still didn't crow. Doodle's beak was sealed.

"It's okay, Doodle," Libby said. "We'll try again tomorrow."

Chapter 3

Rooster Review

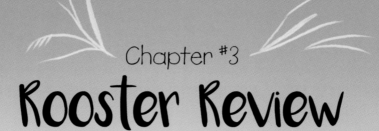

And so early the next morning, Libby went back to the barn for Rooster School.

"Have you practiced crowing, Doodle?" Libby asked.

Doodle flapped his wings. *Peep*!

"No, not peep!" Libby shook her head. "Listen to this."

She pushed play on her CD player. The sounds of crowing roosters filled the barn.

Doodle listened like any good rooster student should. Then Libby pressed stop.

"Got it, Doodle?" Libby asked.

"Now it's your turn."

By then, there was quite a large crowd. The goats, the cows, the pony, and the other chickens had gathered.

They all flocked around Doodle and waited, too.

"Don't be shy, Doodle. Just go for it!" Libby cheered.

Peep! Doodle said.

Libby took a deep breath. "Okay, Doodle, let's review what you *didn't* learn."

Before she could begin, Stewart came into the barn. "How's Rooster School?" he asked.

☐ Cluck
☑ Crow
☐ cock-a-doodle-do

"So far, *not* so good," Libby said.

Stewart had an idea. "Maybe you should act like a chicken."

"You mean, pretend I'm a rooster?" Libby asked.

Stewart nodded.

"It might work," Libby said.

Doodle said, *Peep*!

Chapter #4

Cock-a-Doodle-Won't-Do

"Today, we're trying something new," Libby said at Rooster School the next morning.

Doodle watched as Libby strutted around the barn like a rooster. She scratched in the dirt. She even flapped her arms in the air like wings.

Then Libby cleared her throat and crowed, "Cock-a-doodle-do! Cock-a-doodle-do! Cock-a-doodle-do!"

But Doodle didn't like all of this crowing one bit. He hid behind a bag of corn.

"Doodle, come out!" Libby said. "Please."

Doodle did. *Peep*! he said.

"NO, NO, NO! *Not* peep!" Libby frowned.

Doodle looked into Libby's sad, brown eyes. And Libby looked into Doodle's round rooster eyes.

Peep! Doodle said again.

"I'm sorry, Doodle," Libby said. "Rooster School is canceled!"

Then she stomped into the kitchen where Dad was making pancakes.

"What's wrong?" he asked, stirring the batter.

"Instead of cock-a-doodle-do, it's more like cock-a-doodle-won't-do," Libby said. "Doodle is the worst rooster student ever!"

"Maybe Doodle just needs to grow up a bit," Dad said.

But Libby didn't think so. She was pretty sure Doodle was doomed to a no-crow life.

Chapter #5
5-Star Student

A few days later, Libby and Stewart were catching frogs at the pond.

"Look at this one!" Libby said, stroking the frog's bumpy skin.

"Wow!" Stewart smiled. "He's the biggest one yet."

29

Libby was about to set the frog
on a log when she heard something.
"What was that?" she asked.

"I don't know." Stewart shrugged.

"It's coming from the barn," Libby
said. "Let's go find out."

When they got there, Dad and
Mom were already in the barn.

"What was that sound?" Libby
asked.

Mom pointed at Doodle. "Listen!"

Doodle sat on the gate flapping and flopping his wings.

Libby listened. Stewart did, too.

Then Doodle puffed out his chest. He reared back his head and opened his beak. *Cock-a-doodle-do*!

"Doodle, you did it!" Libby jumped up and down. "You crowed!"

Dad smiled. "I knew he'd do it someday."

Libby smoothed Doodle's feathers. "I was wrong, Doodle. You're the best rooster student ever!" She paused. "But, you're going to have to go back to Rooster School."

"Why is that?" Mom asked.

"Because it isn't morning," Libby sighed. "Now I have to teach Doodle to tell time!"

How Mobile
Devices Are
Changing
Society

Harry Henderson

ReferencePoint
Press®

San Diego, CA

Science, Technology, and Society

About the Author

Harry Henderson has written more than thirty books on science and technology, particularly computing. He lives with his wife, Lisa Yount (a retired writer and active artist), in El Cerrito, California.

For more information, contact:
ReferencePoint Press, Inc.
PO Box 27779
San Diego, CA 92198
www.ReferencePointPress.com

LIBRARY OF CONGRESS CATALOGING-IN-PUBLICATION DATA

Henderson, Harry.
    How mobile devices are changing society / by Harry Henderson.
        pages cm. -- (Science, technology, and society)
    Audience: Grade 9 to 12.
    Includes bibliographical references and index.
    ISBN-13: 978-1-60152-902-2 (hardback)
    ISBN-10: 1-60152-902-3 (hardback)
    1. Information society--Juvenile literature. 2. Wireless communication systems--Juvenile literature. I. Title.
HM851.H46 2015
303.48'33--dc23
                                                                        2015012262

Contents

"Science and technology have had a major impact on society, and their impact is growing. By drastically changing our means of communication, the way we work, our housing, clothes, and food, our methods of transportation, and, indeed, even the length and quality of life itself, science has generated changes in the moral values and basic philosophies of mankind.

"Beginning with the plow, science has changed how we live and what we believe. By making life easier, science has given man the chance to pursue societal concerns such as ethics, aesthetics, education, and justice; to create cultures; and to improve human conditions. But it has also placed us in the unique position of being able to destroy ourselves."

— Donald P. Hearth, former director of the
NASA Langley Research Center, 1985.

Donald P. Hearth wrote these words in 1985. They appear in the foreword of a publication titled *The Impact of Science on Society*, a collection of speeches given during a public lecture series of the same name. Although Hearth's words were written about three decades ago, they are as true today as when they first appeared on the page.

Advances in science and technology undeniably bring about societal change. Gene therapy, for instance, has the potential to revolutionize medicine and the treatment of debilitating illnesses such as sickle-cell anemia and Parkinson's disease. Medical experts say gene therapy might also be used to treat conditions ranging from obesity to depression and someday, perhaps, even to help extend human life spans.

Although gene therapy offers great hope and promise, it also carries significant risks. The 1999 death of an eighteen-year-old patient taking part in a gene therapy clinical trial in the United States provided a painful reminder of the need for strict safeguards and monitoring. Other risks may be less tangible for the time being, but they are no less serious. The idea of changing the genetic instructions for human beings can be construed in some instances as arrogant, immoral, and dangerous. The possibility of making such changes raises questions of who should decide which traits are normal and desirable and which are to be considered unhealthy. It raises questions about the enhancement of the intellectual and athletic capabilities of individuals and about the potential for discrimination against those judged to be in possession of less desirable or faulty genes.

ReferencePoint's *Science, Technology, and Society* series examines scientific and technological advances in the context of their impact on society. Topics covered in the series include gene therapy, the Internet, renewable energy, robotics, and mobile devices. Each book explores how and why this science or technology came about; how it has influenced or shaped daily life and culture; efforts to guide or control the technology through laws and policies; and what the next generation of this technology might look like. Included in the chapters are focus questions aimed at eliciting conversation and debate. Also included are key words and terms and their meanings in the context of the topics covered. Fully documented quotes enliven the narrative and add to the usefulness of the series as a tool for student researchers.

The study of science, technology, and society—sometimes referred to as STS—has gained significant ground in recent years. Top universities, including Stanford and UC Berkeley in California and MIT and Harvard in Massachusetts, are among the many that offer majors or specialized programs devoted to the study of science, technology, and society. The National Science Foundation, an independent federal agency created by Congress in 1950, even has a program that funds research and education specifically on this topic. For secondary students interested in this field, or for those who are merely curious or just trying to fulfill an assignment, ReferencePoint's new series can provide a useful and accessible starting point.

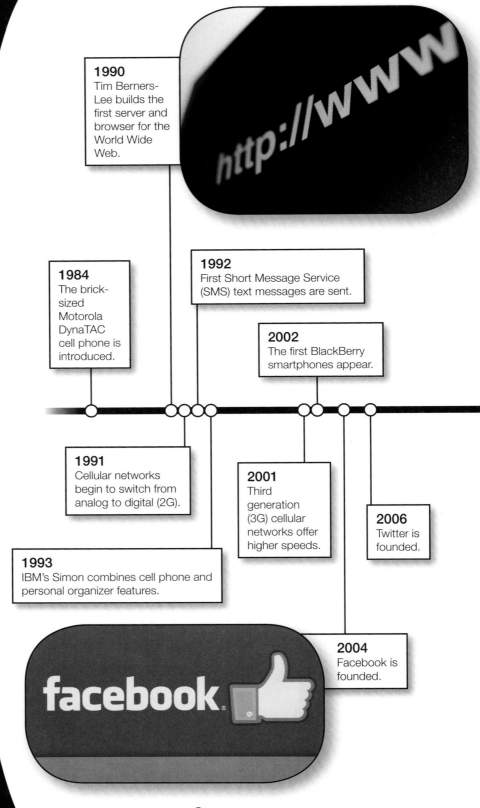

1990
Tim Berners-Lee builds the first server and browser for the World Wide Web.

1984
The brick-sized Motorola DynaTAC cell phone is introduced.

1992
First Short Message Service (SMS) text messages are sent.

2002
The first BlackBerry smartphones appear.

1991
Cellular networks begin to switch from analog to digital (2G).

2001
Third generation (3G) cellular networks offer higher speeds.

2006
Twitter is founded.

1993
IBM's Simon combines cell phone and personal organizer features.

2004
Facebook is founded.

2007
Apple CEO Steve Jobs unveils the iPhone.

2011
Dissidents in Egypt and neighboring countries use cell phones to organize protests.

2010
Apple launches the iPad.

2009
Fourth generation (4G and LTE) cellular networks are introduced.

2013
Google Glass offered to early adopters.

2008
The first Android phones appear.

2012
Large-sized smartphones called "phablets" become popular.

2014
Apple promotes Touch ID fingerprint sensor and Apple Pay.

2015
Apple Watch offers remote control and health-monitoring features.

The Anywhere, Anytime World

Mobile devices have become an integral part of the daily lives of billions of people around the world. By 2012 *Time* magazine writer Richard Stengel had already observed that "the mobile phone has become a kind of super extension of ourselves—faster, brainier, more reliable and always on. . . . There are now more smart phones than toilets in many parts of the world, and the average smart phone today has more computing power than Apollo 11 did when it journeyed to the moon."[1]

The use of mobile devices has continued to expand. According to a 2014 Pew Research survey 90 percent of American adults own a cell phone of some sort, with 64 percent owning a smartphone. Why did mobile devices catch on so quickly and become so widely used? Computer scientist and communications researcher Rich Ling notes that mobile devices, such as the clock in the early industrial era and the automobile in the early twentieth century, are examples of "social mediation technologies." Such technologies become intertwined in many aspects and activities of daily life. He notes that when enough people adopt a new technology, more people find reasons to join in, and social expectations begin to change. As a result, "The adoption of a new technology can challenge the established forms of practice, and it restructures the physical world as it develops into a[n] . . . expected phenomena."[2]

Technology That Has Become Embedded in Society

These factors all play into each other. Just as people often assume that anyone they encounter has access to a car and thus can meet them somewhere without difficulty, people today tend to assume that everyone else has a mobile phone with certain capabilities. For example, it is much less common today for a person making an appointment or inviting someone to a party to provide directions on how to get to the event. It is assumed that the other person will get driving directions from Google Maps or a similar service and will probably have step-by-step real-time navigation help from his or her phone or GPS device as well.

Meanwhile, as people are increasingly expected to have access to the new technology, the holdouts come under increasing pressure to conform. Users of the new devices are quick to point out their latest apps (applications) and what they can do. They may also express frustration when dealing with people who are not yet connected to the always-on network of communications and information. For example, while earlier desktop computer users might check their e-mail only a couple of times a day, in the mobile world people now expect their texts and e-mails to receive a prompt response.

Smartphones and their simpler cell phone counterparts are not the only mobile devices in widespread use today. According to a January 2014 survey by the Pew Research Center, 42 percent of American adults own tablets such as Apple's iPad or popular Android and Windows devices. One of the most popular mobile activities is something people have been doing for centuries—reading. According to the Pew survey, 32 percent of American adults own dedicated e-reader devices such as Amazon's Kindle. Many others can read e-books using

ubiquitous

Widespread, found everywhere.

apps on their smartphones or tablets. The very fact that mobile devices are now so ubiquitous and commonplace can make it hard to appreciate their growing impact. As Ling has observed,

In some ways, the mobile phone is disappearing. I say this knowing that every week many millions of people in India get a mobile phone subscription for the first time. I say it knowing that literally every teen in Denmark and Norway has one. The paradox is, however, that in some interesting ways it is disappearing from our sense of what is remarkable. Mobile communication is becoming embedded in society. It is expected.[3]

Mobile devices have become essential tools of daily living. A 2014 Pew Research Center report that compares survey results over time reveals that American adults have significantly increased their use of mobile devices of all types.

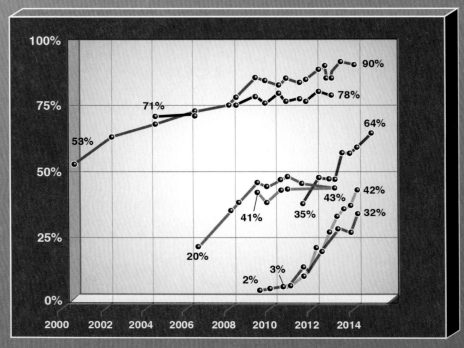

Source: Pew Research Center, "Device Ownership Over Time," Internet & American Life Project, January 2014. www.pewinternet.org.

A Web of Connectivity

Beyond how they have changed daily life, mobile devices are also having a major impact on social and political institutions. Whether in connection with a popular uprising in Egypt or a confrontation between police and protesters in an American city, the images recorded by ubiquitous smartphone cameras often become the center of attention. Mobile devices are empowering do-it-yourself journalism. Other institutions that are being reshaped by the new mobility include education and health care. With their camera-equipped smartphones, students can conduct field research in ecology. Doctors can quickly access electronic medical records, while their patients can track their diet, exercise, and lab tests.

However, even as they empower people in new ways, mobile devices bring new threats to privacy and security. Both the location and the activities of mobile users can be tracked by police or government agencies and by companies seeking to market to consumers. Mobile apps are also vulnerable to malicious software that can steal users' passwords or other sensitive information.

In the face of these developments, social expectations, laws, and government policies are struggling to keep up. Meanwhile, watches, smart eyeglasses, and other wearable devices may represent the next wave of mobility, merging the physical and virtual worlds, weaving themselves into a new web of connectivity.

How Did the World Become Mobile?

In January 2010 Dan Woolley and David Hames had been working in Haiti making a film about that country's extreme poverty. They had just returned to the Hotel Montana in the capital city of Port-au-Prince. But then, as Woolley later told a reporter for *Today*, "I just saw the walls rippling and just explosive sounds all around me. It all happened incredibly fast. David yelled out, 'It's an earthquake,' and we both lunged and everything turned dark."[4]

Woolley's glasses had flown off his face; he felt lost and disoriented in the darkness. The one thing he had handy was an iPhone. He used the phone's camera and flash to light up his surroundings. He saw the bottom of an elevator shaft and decided it would be the safest place to be if another tremor came. However, Woolley was bleeding profusely from wounds on his head and leg. He did not know how badly he had been hurt. He could not call for help because his phone was not receiving a signal.

Woolley thought about what he had on his phone. He called up a first aid app. Following its instructions, he used his shirt and a sock to fashion a tourniquet and bandage for his leg and a bandage for his head wound. Because the app warned him that he might go into shock and fall asleep, he set the phone's alarm to go off every twenty minutes. After that all he could do was wait. He spent the time recording voice messages for his wife and sons. Sometimes he listened to music stored on his phone. When the battery level dropped to 20 percent, he shut off the phone to save power. Finally, after sixty-five hours he heard the sounds of a rescue party breaking through.

Without his smartphone it is doubtful Woolley could have lived long enough to be rescued. This versatile device, even when it could not function as a telephone, could nevertheless be a camera, a flashlight, a medical adviser, and hundreds of other useful things. It took a number of intertwining technologies to finally put this tiny but powerful machine in people's pockets and purses.

The First Mobile Telephones

Around the time of World War II people had radio telephones, including backpack-sized radios and slightly smaller walkie-talkies. These were not like modern cell phones. Users could only connect to a single other device or to a base station that connected to a limited number of subscribers.

Later in the 1940s the first mobile telephones began to be installed in cars, and they were connected through AT&T's Mobile Telephone Service. All calls had to be made through an operator, and only a few connections could be made at a time. Car phones were very expensive and were considered to be a status symbol for executives and a few other people who had to be able to communicate while on the road.

transceiver

A device that can both send and receive communications or data.

About ten years later the noted science fiction writer and futurist Arthur C. Clarke wrote an article in which he envisioned "a personal transceiver, so small and compact that every man carries one." Clarke foresaw that "the time will come when we will be able to call a person anywhere on Earth merely by dialing a number." Clarke even predicted that the phone would be able to determine its current position so that "no one need ever again be lost."[5]

Building a wireless phone system that could connect anyone to anyone else virtually anywhere would require developing a very different kind of network. Existing radio telephones worked by connecting subscribers to a central radio tower in each city. Each person connecting needed his or her own frequency, and only a couple of dozen or so frequencies were available.

The cellular system that began to be developed in the 1970s works on a different principle. Instead of one tower and a handful of frequencies, it uses many small towers covering areas called cells. Because the range between the user and the nearest cell is just a few miles at most, much lower power can be used, allowing multiple users to employ the same frequency without interfering with one another. The cells in each city for each provider's system are coordinated by a Mobile Telephone Switching Office (MTSO). The MTSO also handles the connections between cell users and the regular landline phone system. (This is why a person can use a cell phone to call a landline.)

Each cell phone has a unique identifying code that it broadcasts. As the user moves from one cell to another (perhaps in a car), the MTSO keeps track of which cell the phone is in. If the phone gets out of range of its current cell, it is switched over to the

An early mobile car phone, demonstrated in 1946, comes with a dial on the car's dashboard for making calls. Because they were expensive, few people during this time period owned mobile phones.

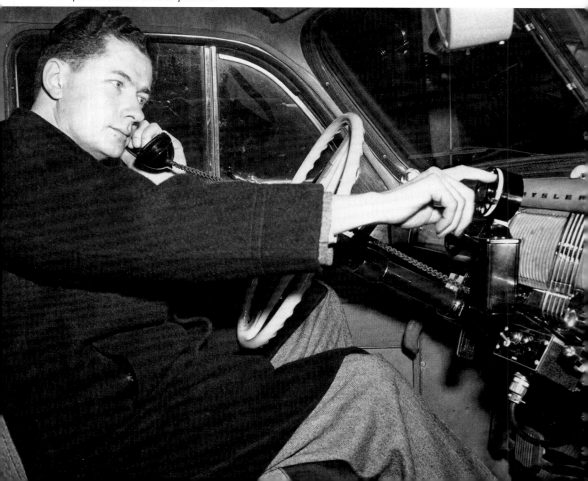

cell that has the strongest signal, usually without interrupting the call. However, in some areas (usually remote and sparsely populated) where there is no signal the phone shows the dreaded "no service" message.

The Growth of Cellular Networks

The switch from analog (first generation or 1G) cellular systems to digital (second generation or 2G) in the 1990s allowed systems to accommodate the growing number of users, as well as allowing more data to be transmitted. This is because digital signals, like other digital data, can be manipulated by computers. In one system, called TDMA, each piece of data is compressed so it only takes a third as much time to transmit—meaning a frequency can handle three times as many calls.

Another widely used approach, called CDMA, "stamps" each piece of signal with a unique sequence code and sends it over the next available frequency. At the receiving phone the relevant pieces are identified and stitched back together. All this happens so fast one normally does not hear a delay.

packets

"Chunks" of data on the Internet or similar networks. They can be sent to specific addresses and reassembled into complete files.

The method used in CDMA, called spread spectrum, is rather like the way the Internet works. On the Internet data is broken up into identifiable "packets" that are sent over an appropriate connection and then reassembled at the destination computer. Indeed, at the very time when cell phone service was being designed and implemented, the Internet was also coming of age. With the development of the smartphone, the two technologies would be married into a device that could take full advantage of both.

It All Comes Together

Cell phones grew rapidly in popularity as the 1990s drew to an end. The adoption of mobile phones was accelerated by a new business model. Just as in the early twentieth century Kodak made its cameras popular by selling the devices cheaply and making money on film and developing, phone providers began to sell phones cheaply. In return, the buyer agreed to a service contract lasting for a period such as two years. Today the same sort of plan makes it possible to buy a smartphone with a stand-alone price of $600 for only $200 up front. The remaining $400 is folded into the monthly service payments.

Cell phones were not the only portable devices that were becoming popular in the latter part of the century. People have always enjoyed the idea of having devices they could carry around with them and use anywhere. In the 1950s transistor radios provided music at the beach or at a picnic. Later came small cassette recorders. In the 1980s the Sony Walkman was a big hit. One could pop in a cassette and listen to the music on personally assembled mix tapes while jogging. By the 1990s the music had migrated to CDs and digital MP3 files, even as the devices continued to shrink in size. In 2001 Apple introduced the iPod. The iPod was not the first digital music player, but its clear display and easy to use click wheel menus made it easy to create playlists and control the playback and volume. In 2003 Apple added iTunes, an online store that made it easy to buy and download music tracks.

Meanwhile, laptop computers became popular in the 1990s and gradually became lighter and more powerful. However, while a laptop was portable, it could not be pulled out of a pocket and used to look up an address or make a quick note. During these same years a new kind of small, portable device called the PDA (personal digital assistant, or personal data assistant) became popular. A PDA made it possible to manage one's calendar, appointments, contacts, and notes while accessing e-mail and browsing the Web to a limited extent. By the end of the decade PDAs from Palm and BlackBerry became familiar accessories for many businesspeople.

Birth of the Smartphone

One big problem with these personal organizer devices was that they could not be used to make phone calls. A phone number could be looked up in the PDA's address book, but then the user would have to take out a separate cell phone to make the call.

Smartphones and Science Fiction

Starting more than half a century ago, two celebrated science fiction writers saw cell phones—and smartphones—coming. In Robert Heinlein's 1948 novel *Space Cadet* the young protagonist is on his way to the spaceport. He pulls a phone out of his pocket and calls his father. He then arranges to ship the phone home before going into space, where the device could not get a signal. By 1976 science fiction writer and futurist Arthur C. Clarke was predicting what would become the smartphone:

> We're going to get devices which will enable us to send much more information to our friends. They're going to be able to see us, we're going to see them, we're going to exchange pictorial information, graphical information, data, books, and so forth.

> You can call in through this any information you might want: airline flights, the price of things at the supermarket, books you've always wanted to read, news you've selectively [chosen]. The machine will hunt and bring this all to you, selectively.

> Predicting Skype, e-readers, Google, and what amounts to the Web is rather impressive, particularly since the first cell phone systems were barely on the drawing board.

Arthur C. Clarke, interview, AT&T/MIT Conference, 1976. www.youtube.com.

The next logical step was to combine the PDA and the cell phone into a single, more versatile device. In 1993 IBM introduced the Simon Personal Communicator, the first device that could be called a smartphone. Besides making phone calls, the user could send faxes and e-mails. Other built-in applications included an address book, calendar, appointment scheduler, and notepad.

The Simon sold only about fifty thousand units, however. By modern standards it was bulky—brick-shaped, 8 inches (20 cm) long, and weighed more than a pound (450 g). Its developer, IBM, had ruled the mainframe world since the 1960s and had pretty much set the standards for desktop personal computers (PCs).

However, by the later 1990s IBM was no longer in the forefront of consumer electronics.

Cell phone makers who were supplying growing networks—particularly in Japan and Europe—were better poised to enter the smartphone market. One of the leaders in this early smartphone market was Nokia, whose Communicator 9110 flipped open to reveal a keyboard and screen and offered a primitive Web browser. This and similar smartphones were popular abroad, but the lack of suitable cell networks continued to slow the adoption of cell phones and smartphones in the United States until the turn of the new century.

The first widely popular smartphone in the United States was the BlackBerry, introduced in 2003. This device integrated phone, e-mail, text messaging, and Web browsing and supplied a thumb-friendly, real keyboard. People seemed to become addicted to checking their e-mail on the device, leading to the term "crack-berry."

Apple Reinvents the Smartphone

While the BlackBerry was a hit with many businesspeople and professionals, it took a pioneering computer company to make the smartphone a true consumer product. Apple did not invent the personal computer, but the company made it easier to use with the Macintosh (introduced in 1984) and its icon-based operating system. Apple did not invent the digital media player either, but the easy to use iPod soon took over the market. In 2007 Apple was ready to reinvent another technology. CEO Steve Jobs made the announcement: "Today, we're introducing three revolutionary products. An iPod, a phone, and an Internet communicator. An iPod, a phone—Are you getting it? These are not three separate devices. This is one device. We're calling it iPhone."[6]

One thing that made the iPhone so successful was its simplicity. The compact, light phone had few buttons. Users simply touched icons on the screen to access applications, or swiped their fingers across the screen. Typing was done using an on-screen keyboard. Virtually all smartphones and tablets developed since then would feature a touch interface.

Steve Jobs introduces Apple's new iPhone at a conference in 2007. Apple did not invent the smartphone, but its innovations influenced nearly all subsequent smartphone designs.

While Apple's share of the smartphone market would remain modest (usually varying between 15 and 20 percent), its control of the hardware and of software distribution channels would make the device very profitable, accounting for more than half the company's total revenue. Perhaps more significantly, Apple's influence over the design of modern smartphones and tablets is unmistakable.

Apps—a New Kind of Software

Another innovation by Apple led to the runaway success of the iPhone and its competitors. It has to do not with hardware, design, or user interface but with a new model for the development and

Buying the First Cell Phone

Even way back in 1984 one could buy a cell phone—that is, if one had $3,995 to spare (or about $9,025 in 2015 dollars). That was the price for a Motorola DynaTAC 8000X, the first commercially available cell phone. It certainly would not fit in a pocket, though. The device measured 13 by 1.75 by 3.5 inches (33 x 4.5 x 8.9 cm) and weighed a hefty 28 ounces (795 g). It had a battery life of only thirty minutes. It had only one use—to make and receive phone calls. Paul Gudonis, the CEO of Ameritech, which was building the first cellular network in the Chicago area at the time, said market research suggested that cell phone buyers would be "a select group of entrepreneurs, doctors, real estate agents, construction company owners and large company executives."

It would be more than a decade before most teenagers and their parents would have cell phones, but the devices caught on rapidly with businesspeople and workers who had to go out into the field where there might not be a landline phone for miles. Motorola's Rudolf Krolopp, who designed the DynaTAC and later devices, noted that "we didn't design them for teenagers—well, unless it was a teenager with $4,000."

Quoted in Stewart Wolpin, "The First Cellphone Went on Sale 30 Years Ago for $4,000," Mashable.com, March 13, 2014. http://mashable.com.

---

sale of software. Installing new software on a personal computer during the last century was a cumbersome task that involved physical disks or CDs, user manuals, and performing configuration steps that often were hard to understand. Users also had to be aware of frequent "patches" or updates needed in order to keep the software running properly.

Software for mobile devices is very different. It comes in the form of apps. Users of Apple, Android, and Windows mobile devices can browse an app store with hundreds of thousands of apps. Unlike traditional software many apps are free, and many others cost only a few dollars. It takes only a couple of touches to buy, download, and install an app. Running an app is just as easy. Any time an app is updated the new version can be installed with just a touch or even automatically. Although all modern mobile devices are based on the use of apps, technology writer Brian X. Chen has noted that Apple was the pioneer in making all the pieces (apps, developers, devices, consumers) work together:

> Everything about the iPhone and the App Store was designed to fit an always-on, mobile lifestyle. So Apple did not invent something brand new out of necessity and thereby lift off a revolution. After all, so much of what apps can do has been doable for years. Instead, Apple's [way of operating] has traditionally been to study an existing technology and determine how it can be done better.[7]

As industry analyst Mark Mulligan has commented, "Apps have transformed consumers' expectations of what digital experiences should be, and not just on connected devices." As a result, Mulligan believes that "apps have created a renaissance in the consumer software market."[8] Generally speaking, apps are easier to create than traditional programs. Some apps simply present existing websites in a way that is better suited to small devices, such as reformatting a newspaper to make it more readable on a tablet. However, mobile operating systems provide many resources that programmers can hook into when creating software, including hardware such as the built-in camera and microphone or the GPS device that reports the user's location. Meanwhile numerous services such as Google Maps provide a wealth of additional data that can be tapped by app developers to create new features and services. For example, an "eating out" app might take restaurant reviews from the popular Yelp review site, access a Google map of the user's neighborhood, and show which highly rated restaurants are within easy walking or driving distance.

Bridging the Technological Gap

Even though mobile devices are easier to use than traditional computers, and their features and apps are often attractive, there have been differences in how rapidly different groups of people have been able to take advantage of them. This poses a social challenge that first emerged with the advent of the personal computer a generation earlier. As the use of personal computers and the Internet grew in the 1990s, there was an accompanying concern about a digital divide between the educated middle class who had access to the new technology and those groups who were in danger of being left behind. Factors that make it harder for people to participate in the digital world include poverty, lack of basic knowledge about technology, language barriers, and sometimes age or disability.

digital divide

The difficulty that certain groups of people have with adopting and using new computer technologies.

In some ways mobile devices have begun to bridge the digital divide. A 2013 Pew Center report, "The State of Digital Divides," notes that between 2011 and 2013 American smartphone ownership increased from 35 percent to 56 percent. During this time 15 percent of blacks and 22 percent of Hispanics achieved broadband access not through home connections but by obtaining a smartphone.

Mobile devices can be an attractive way to begin participating in online life. They are designed to be easy and convenient to use, and they require little setup or maintenance. Smartphones also include Web browsers and applications that make it possible to take advantage of many Web-based services without having to buy a traditional PC. However, the plans offered by phone providers can be complicated, expensive, or offer limited amounts of data; and signal strength and speed can vary by neighborhood. Their relatively small screens and keyboards make mobile devices less suitable for reading or working with large amounts of text. Thus students who do not have personal computers and Internet connections at home will continue to be at a disadvantage in studying or doing homework.

Other services may not be available to people who have only a phone connection to the Internet. Susan Crawford, a professor at Harvard's Kennedy School of Government, notes that "there just isn't adequate bandwidth to hold a video conference call or get an education or get access to telemedicine. None of that is realistically possible over a wireless connection on a smartphone."[9] Many web-

Who Owns Smartphones?

Smartphone ownership in the United States is widespread, especially among young adults and adults with high incomes and high levels of education, according to a 2015 report by the Pew Research Center. When compared with past surveys, ownership in all categories is rising.

Percent of US Adults in Each Group Who Owns a Smartphone

All adults	**64%**
Male	66%
Female	63%
18–29	85%
30–49	79%
50–64	54%
65+	27%
White, non-Hispanic	61%
Black, non-Hispanic	70%
Hispanic	71%
HS grad or less	52%
Some college	69%
College+	78%
Less than $30,000/yr	50%
$30,000–$49,999	71%
$50,000–$74,999	72%
$75,000 or more	84%
Urban	68%
Suburban	66%
Rural	52%

Source: Pew Research Center, "Smartphone Ownership Highest Among Young Adults, Those with High Income/Education Levels," Internet & American Life Project, March 31, 2015.

sites that people use to seek health care, government services, or employment are still not formatted for mobile devices, making them difficult to use. However, some of these drawbacks may be addressed by the emergence of mobile devices that combine some of the advantages of the smartphone with the desktop or laptop PC.

Mobile Evolution Continues

The ease of use and versatility of smartphones is attractive, but there are applications and activities that seem to need a larger screen and keyboard area. Using the same operating system as the iPhone and its lightweight and sleek design, Apple introduced the iPad in 2010. The iPad was not the first tablet computer (Apple itself had introduced a slate-like computer called the Newton in 1993). However, the new touch interface, faster processors, and the burgeoning market of apps made the iPad a far more capable and popular device.

Other tablets based on Google's Android operating system or on versions of Microsoft Windows would also become popular. Despite differences in cameras, screens, and overall design touted by their fans, tablets—like smartphones—are much more similar than they are different. For one thing, all of them connect to the same Web with its Facebook, Twitter, YouTube, and other popular services.

After the burst of innovation represented by the iPhone and iPad, development of these devices has been more evolutionary than revolutionary. Screen resolution continues to increase, and designers are beginning to introduce 3-D features. Cameras have become more capable, eliminating the need for most people to carry a separate point-and-shoot camera. With multi-core processors, some tablets begin to approach the power and capability of laptops, making them more suitable for creating documents and performing other office tasks.

The next wave of the mobile revolution seems to be coming in the form of new kinds of wearable devices such as watches and eyeglass-mounted devices. While it is too early to tell whether these items or others will catch on in the way smartphones and tablets have done, there is no doubt that new capabilities and applications will continue to emerge.

Chapter Two

Mobile Devices and Daily Life

Focus Questions

1. How is young people's experience of the digital world today different from that of their parents' in the 1990s?
2. People seem to be aware that distracted driving is dangerous, but many continue to use their devices while on the road. What might account for this behavior?
3. What are some things to consider before downloading an app?

"Technology can be our best friend, and technology can also be the biggest party pooper of our lives. It interrupts our own story, interrupts our ability to have a thought or a daydream, to imagine something wonderful, because we're too busy bridging the walk from the cafeteria back to the office on the cell phone."

— Steven Spielberg, prominent American filmmaker.

Quoted in Lester D. Friedman, *Citizen Spielberg*. Urbana, IL: University of Illinois, 2006, p. 145.

By the beginning of the twenty-first century, computers and the Internet were already playing an increasingly important role in people's lives. Amazon was reshaping the retail industry—selling not just books but hundreds of other products. eBay had created a vast market in which people could offer or buy just about any legal product. Google's powerful search engine was delivering answers to billions of queries along with targeted advertising.

Only one thing was preventing the digital world from penetrating every aspect of daily life. To search for something, to send an e-mail or post a message, or to buy something, one had to physically go to a computer and go online. (People spoke of logging on, surfing the Web, and then logging off.) Even laptop computers, though portable, had to be opened, set down somewhere, and booted up, which made it hard to follow a spontaneous impulse to find something online.

Mobile devices—smartphones and tablets—would change all that. They are always at hand, always just a touch or button press away. One can use them just about anywhere.

Always Connected

Being always connected makes it easier to do all the things people were trying to do online in the 1990s, but it also makes new kinds of activities possible or practicable. In particular, faster and easier access to relevant information has increased the pace and efficiency of commerce and industry. Mobile tech entrepreneur Michael Saylor observes:

entrepreneur

A person who develops and implements new forms of business.

> It's easy to underestimate the power of information. Mobile technology puts real time information in your pocket, allowing everyone to magnify his or her knowledge in any setting. In the hands of business executives we see faster and smarter decision making. In the hands of consumers we see smarter buying. . . . In the hands of third world farmers we see much more efficient markets.[10]

Besides the ease of getting instant information, Saylor also notes that social networks such as Facebook are another big draw for phone use:

What amplifies the transformational power ahead is the confluence of two major technological currents today: the universal access to mobile computing and the pervasive use of social networks. Social networks radically increase the use of computing devices, and mobile computing increases the usefulness of social software. It's a virtuous cycle that magnifies the impact of both waves.[11]

Multitasking

The downside of being always connected is that one is always being interrupted. Tech blogger Joe Colton calls smartphones "the most pervasive interruption technology ever." Writing in 2011, he recalled that "just 15 years ago, interruption technology was mostly confined to the land line telephone. People used this interruption technology sparingly, calling businesses and homes at 'reasonable' hours. And many people had rules for keeping interruptions to a minimum, such as my parents' rule of not answering the phone during dinner." All this has now changed, Colton explains:

> Most people carry a cell phone at all times. Voice calls are now just one small part of an ongoing stream of interruptions. Many people set their phones to alert them for each incoming text, instant message, calendar event, and/or e-mail. Some go further with social status notifications from Twitter or Facebook, while others may want to be alerted every time a friend is nearby or their favorite team gets a score.[12]

As if that were not enough, Colton observes, people have gotten in the habit of constantly checking their phone for updates of various sorts. "It's all too tempting to frequently check (or 'pull') weather, scores, stock prices, etc. Many people elect to keep pushed interruptions to a minimum, but then obsessively check their smartphone. Whether self-induced or pushed, an interruption is an interruption,"[13] says Colton.

This scene, photographed in London in 2015, is a common sight in cities around the world. People of all ages, not just teens, are constantly on their phones—and almost none of that time is actually spent making calls.

All these interactions with the mobile device mean that people often seem to be doing several things simultaneously. This is called multitasking. Actually, the term is a bit misleading. The human vision and attention systems can only look at one thing or perform one activity at a time. The brain is constantly switching between tasks—and there may be limits to how well that works. Stanford professor Clifford Nass studied multitasking among students and concluded that "we have evidence that high multitaskers are worse at managing their short-term memory and worse at switching tasks."[14]

Other experts, such as Mark Liberman of the linguistics blog Language Log, question these results. Liberman observes that the heavy multitaskers might be people who are already easily distracted, rather than having been made so by their devices. Liberman does agree that "if it's really true that modern digital multitasking causes significant cognitive disability and even brain damage

. . . then many very serious social and individual changes are urgently needed."[15]

Multitasking is not a new phenomenon, however. Stay-at-home parents will be especially familiar with this concept. Vaughan Bell, a neuropsychologist at the Universidad de Antioquia, Colombia, points out: "If you think Twitter is an attention magnet, try living with an infant. Kids are the most distracting thing there is, and when you have three or even four in the house it is both impossible to focus on one thing—and stressful, because the consequences of not keeping an eye on your kids can be frightening even to think about."[16]

multitasking

Shifting one's attention rapidly between different activities.

Dangerous Distractions

It might be possible for people to learn how to cope with multitasking in a digital world. But what happens when one of the activities is one in which inattention can have serious or even fatal consequences?

On September 22, 2006, nineteen-year-old Reggie Shaw seemed to be unaware that his sport utility vehicle was weaving over the yellow center line as he went over a mountain pass near Logan, Utah. His SUV then clipped a car that was traveling in the other direction. The other car spun out and crossed the road, where it was broadsided by a truck and trailer. The car's driver and passenger, both well-respected scientists working on rocket boosters, were killed.

Shaw, on the other hand, was unhurt. When asked about the accident, he repeatedly said he did not know how it happened—that perhaps the car had skidded on the icy road. Prosecutors eventually came to a different conclusion. Phone records showed that Shaw had sent or received eleven text messages around the time of the crash. It was unclear what charges would be laid against Shaw, since at the time no law specifically forbade texting while driving. Struggling to come to terms with his responsibility for the tragedy, Shaw made a plea agreement and served a short jail term. He then began to visit schools, telling students about what he had done, the consequences he had to face, and the fact that he could never make up for the two lives that had been taken. He tells his young audience, "I'm here for one reason. That's for you guys to look at me and say: I don't want to be that guy."[17]

Distracted driving (particularly involving texting or smartphone use) is a major cause of traffic accidents. In 2012 the federal government estimated that 3,328 deaths and 421,000 injuries resulted from accidents in which drivers were distracted. Adding to the problem is the fact that young people ages sixteen to nineteen are avid mobile device users but inexperienced drivers.

Regulators have tried to address the problem. While no federal laws have been passed, thirty-nine states and the District of Columbia have passed laws with varying restrictions on use of mobile devices while driving. In some cases hands-free devices are required for voice calling, and most states have banned texting while driving. However, studies have suggested that it is not distracted

A freeway sign reminds California drivers that the use of a hands-free cell phone while driving is legal but a handheld cell phone is not. Distracted driving, specifically tied to cell phone use, has become a major road hazard in many states.

eyes but distracted minds that are the biggest problem. Further, laws governing mobile device use are seldom enforced and are a low priority for police. Educational programs including videos have been used by federal and state agencies to try to convey the dangers of distracted driving, but their effectiveness is unclear.

Technology introduces new distractions, but technology can also help people focus their attention on what matters. Even as cars get more elaborate navigation, control, and entertainment systems, auto designers can try to minimize driver distraction and keep drivers' eyes on the road. Some cars can already detect and avoid potential collisions. Perhaps in ten to twenty years the widespread use of self-driving cars might turn everyone into a passenger and eliminate the problem.

Growing Up Connected

Issues such as how to discourage distracted driving also highlight differences between generations and how they relate to mobile devices. The adults who largely run the world today grew up in the mid- to late-twentieth century. Their exposure to computing was limited; back then the online world was primitive, and mobile devices were not yet part of daily life. A younger generation sees mobile devices quite differently. Millennials (people born around the turn of the twenty-first century) are now in their teens or early adulthood. They grew up in families that

millennial

A person born around the turn of the twenty-first century.

were connecting to the Internet. They have probably spent many hours with consoles and online games and quickly take to each new device that is introduced. This generation is already making its desires and perspectives felt, particularly in the tech industry, which is dominated by young adults.

Even the way people use the same sort of technology can differ between generations. While adults (even seniors) eventually came to embrace Facebook, the youngsters favor Twitter and Instagram and even newer social networks. A popular social networking app in colleges and high schools today is Yik Yak. This app creates an anonymous network within a limited area (such as a school) where people can post whatever they want without being identified. Unfortunately, while being anonymous may help shy people express themselves, it also means that harassment and cyberbullying have free rein. A number of colleges and high schools have banned use of the app on their campuses. The app's developers have responded by including geo-fences that block the app from working within specified geographical boundaries.

As adults and young people try to negotiate the use of mobile devices, each group needs to realize that the experience and viewpoint of the other group may be quite different. Adults tend to see the new technology as a useful way to enhance the social relationships they have built up over the years and to make new contacts. For young people, however, texting, photo sharing, and other forms of social networking are simply how one *is* social today.

geo-fence

Software that prevents an app from functioning within a particular area, such as a school.

Digital Drugs?

As smartphones became an integral part of young people's social lives, concerns arose about a new kind of addiction — not to alcohol, tobacco, or other drugs, but to electronic devices. First the focus was on television when it was observed that young people were spending more time in front of the TV screen than they spent in school. Next came video games, which came with the added concern about violent content. However, TV and desktop computers have a fixed location. They cannot be brought to school or used on the playground. It is different with smartphones and other handheld devices, which can be pulled out of a pocket anywhere.

James Roberts, a marketing professor at Baylor University, asked college students how much time they spent with their phone each day. The answer was a mind-boggling nine hours. Some students agreed that "I spend more time than I should on my cell phone," and others agreed that "I get agitated when my phone is not in sight."[18] Other statements suggest that students used their phones and social networks when they wanted to lift

"Breathing the Mobile Technology"

In *The Mobile Wave* Michael Saylor suggests that "mobile technology is changing the nature of software. It's causing software to transform from a 'solid form' to a 'vapor form.'" . . . He suggests:

> To fully grasp the new gas-like nature of mobile software, visit a shopping mall and observe a group of teenagers. In a group of four, you might see one person talking, one listening, one texting, and the fourth connected to the Internet on her phone. Yet these teenagers will all be engaged in the same conversation. The texter is extending the conversation to distant friends. The one on the Internet is posting the conversation to a Facebook page, as well as checking the time of the movie they intend to see. These teenagers are breathing the mobile technology that is available to them. They are using it as an integral part of their immediate social activity.

People who grow up using computer technology are sometimes called "digital natives." This refers to how they use technology fluently as though speaking their native language. For older people, learning new technology may be more like learning a second language. Such a language can be mastered but is unlikely to be as fluent and effortless.

Michael Saylor, *The Mobile Wave: How Mobile Intelligence Will Change Everything.* Boston: Da Capo, 2012, p. 9.

their mood. Some found that they needed an increasing amount of phone time in order to feel properly connected. These experiences seem similar to those of a drug addict who needs to take more and more of the drug in order to feel good.

Not everyone who uses a smartphone regularly will experience addictive behavior, but it does happen. One sign of a problem may be excessive stress or anxiety relieved only temporarily by checking for messages and updates. Another warning sign is frequently "tuning out" of face-to-face conversations with family or friends.

Writing in the health website WebMD, experts suggest some ways to manage one's phone use to avoid such problems:

- **Be conscious** of the situations and emotions that make you want to check your phone. Is it boredom? Loneliness? Anxiety? Maybe something else would soothe you.

- **Be strong** when your phone beeps or rings. You don't always have to answer it. In fact, you can avoid temptation by turning off the alert signals.

- **Be disciplined** about not using your device in certain situations (such as when you're with . . . children, driving, or in a meeting) or at certain hours (for instance, between 9 p.m. and 7 a.m.)[19]

Making Choices About Privacy

Besides the risk of developing an unhealthy attachment or addiction, frequent use of mobile devices exposes people to the everyday privacy risks of the online world—and to some less familiar ones as well. In recent years there has been much publicity about how popular websites use information about people's online browsing. After all, the many useful free services that are provided by Google, Yahoo!, and other major Web companies have to be paid for somehow. Generally the revenue comes from advertising—specifically, by using information about users' interests and selections to sell targeted ads. While most users have become aware that much information about them can be gleaned online, they may not be aware of how the thousands of apps on their mobile devices can also obtain and share information. In a 2013 report Hewlett-Packard Corporation (HP) asks whether apps should be able to access so much of the data stored on a typical smartphone:

Should the newest version of the game Mad Mallards have access to text your contact list or sent e-mail? Or actually

34

be able to call a telephone number? What if it wanted to send your contact list to a third party website? We found that a whopping 97 percent of applications had access to and were able to share this type of data. . . . We found banking apps that integrated with social media, chat apps that sent chat logs to be analyzed for future purchasing trends, and many, many applications that track you via geo-location.[20]

Having scooped up sensitive personal data, many apps do not safeguard it from hackers who might want it for purposes more nefarious than targeting ads. The HP researchers found that 86 percent of the apps surveyed did not include basic security measures to prevent them from being compromised by attackers. The HP report also learned that 75 percent of the apps did not encrypt the data they stored on users' devices to render it useless if stolen.

Since apps are made by thousands of separate developers rather than a few large software companies, it will not be easy to regulate them. The big app stores from Google, Microsoft, and particularly Apple establish rules for app developers about how they can use a device's capabilities and access internal data. Apps that break the rules can be pulled from sale. However, restrictions can also prevent innovation by making it impossible for a developer to implement certain features.

There are indications that mobile device users are becoming increasingly concerned about privacy and perhaps becoming more careful about the apps they use. A 2013 report from the California Attorney General's office notes: "Clearly, many consumers find value in mobile apps and are eager to try new ones as they are released. But many of these same consumers are concerned about privacy. A recent study found that more than half of mobile app users had uninstalled or decided not to install an app because of concerns about its privacy practices."[21]

Working together with major app platform companies such as Apple, Google, and Amazon, the California Attorney General has developed recommendations and guidelines for the app industry. In general, app developers are urged to carefully consider what sort of user information is truly needed for a given app and how it will be safeguarded. Privacy policies should be clear, but users should also be alerted when they are being asked to share information beyond what would be expected. Controls used to specify privacy settings should be understandable and easy to use.

They Know Where You Are

Another kind of sensitive information is unique to mobile devices. Because smartphones have built-in GPS locators, apps such as the ubiquitous Google Maps can use this data to provide location-specific information such as where in the neighborhood to get a pizza. Of course, people are always looking for other people, too, particularly friends. An app called Swarm allows users to check into a location so that other people in their social network know they are there.

These apps are changing the way people plan their social activities. Traditionally, one might set the time and place for a party and then invite people to come. With mobile apps, people who have some free time may be more inclined to spontaneously decide to get together without having to plan in advance.

Social networks can be very useful for keeping in touch with friends and for finding new social opportunities. However, many people post extensive publicly accessible information about themselves on Facebook and other services. When an app combines location information with the ability to display personal details, the results can be quite creepy, as writer John Brownlee found. An app called Girls Around Me plots a radar-like map around the user's location and displays the pictures of women who had checked into the area using Foursquare, a popular location-based social network. Clicking on a picture brings up detailed information drawn from the person's Facebook profile, which is likely to include where she went to school, where she works, and her interests. (While the app can be used by women to find men, the default settings and marketing images focus on men seeking women.)

Defenders of apps like Girls Around Me see them as clever ways to combine existing information and give more people opportunities to meet someone compatible. However, Girls Around

House Rules for the Mobile Age

Every family has its rules, whether they are spelled out or not. One tech blogger has suggested some general rules for mobile devices that could be worth trying. One rule is to not allow devices during meals, since that may be one of the few times family members actually sit together face-to-face. Similarly, if the family goes out to a restaurant or movie together, they should put their phones away and enjoy one another's company.

Beyond those daily events, she suggests that some special deviceless days be designated: "There will be days, events, outings and holidays when we all commit to being device-free. Sometimes it feels nice to go for a walk without bringing the hundreds of people we know along with us. Even if it's virtually."

She also urges that unexpected opportunities for direct human contact not be missed: "A visitor stops by. A conversation forms. Friends gather. Humans in real life always take priority over humans in online life. It's just better for everyone that way."

Janell Burley Hofmann, "Our 'Slow Tech' Family iRules," The Blog (*Huffington Post*), December 30, 2014. www.huffingtonpost.com.

Me does not require that women sign up with the app and agree to have their profiles exposed on it. As Brownlee explains, "The settings determining how visible your Facebook and Foursquare data is are complicated, and tend to be meaningless to people who don't really understand issues about privacy. Most privacy settings on social networks default to share everything with everyone, and since most people never change those . . . well, they end up getting sucked up into apps like this.[22]

Although Foursquare cut off access to its check-in data and Apple removed it from its app store, the app was soon back in a slightly altered form. As Brownlee noted, the real problem exposed by apps such as Girls Around Me is that people do not realize that the information they choose to expose in one context (such as a Facebook profile) can be freely combined with all sorts of other information to enable strangers to know much more about them than one might imagine. Although Facebook recently improved its privacy control settings, it remains very difficult for the average person to know who can access their information on social networks and what limitations (if any) there might be on what can be done with that information.

As smartphone ownership spreads among younger kids, this new vulnerability extends to children. In 2012 the Federal Trade Commission (FTC) issued a report that notes the tremendous growth in mobile apps and observes, "Consumers have down-loaded these apps more than 28 billion times, and young children and teens are increasingly embracing smartphone technology for entertainment and educational purposes."[23] The kind of informa-tion that many mobile apps gather, such as the user's precise location, phone number, and list of contacts, can make children particularly vulnerable. The report urges that app developers, app stores, and service providers ensure that parents have appropriate privacy information in an understandable form.

Smartphones: Should They Need a Warrant?

Apps and advertisers are not the only people who might be in-terested in what is on one's device. Few people realize just how much sensitive information is now routinely carried in their pock-ets. A typical smartphone will have the names and numbers of one's frequent contacts, appointments, stored e-mails or text messages, notes, copies of documents, and much more.

This information would be of great interest if one becomes the subject of a police investigation. It has long been normal and per-missible for the police, when arresting someone, to look through the contents of their pockets, such as wallets. Such a search was justified by the need to secure any weapons the suspect might have and to prevent him or her from destroying evidence.

The question raised by the new technology is whether the much more detailed digital contents of a mobile device should also be obtainable without a warrant. If a phone now contains as much data as a whole office might have housed in the past, should not the Fourth Amendment's statement that "the right of the people to be secure in their persons, houses, papers, and effects, against unreasonable searches and seizures" come into play? In the 2014 case of *Riley v. California*, which involved the police search of a cell phone seized during an arrest, the US Supreme Court noted that "modern cell phones are not just another technological convenience. With all they contain and all they may reveal, they hold for many Americans 'the privacies of life.' The fact that technology now allows an individual to carry such information in his hand does not make the information any less worthy of the protection for which the Founders fought."[24]

In this landmark decision the Court ruled that police must get a warrant before seizing and examining the contents of a suspect's cell phone. However, the balance between privacy and law

A Los Angeles police officer checks the cell phone of a man who has been detained. Because modern cell phones contain so much personal information, the US Supreme Court ruled that police must obtain a warrant before seizing and searching a person's cell phone.

enforcement for mobile device users continues to evolve. For example, a number of police departments are now using a device called a StingRay to track cell phone users and even listen in on their conversations. Eventually courts and legislators will have to decide what restrictions if any should be placed on such surveillance devices. Thus, as mobile devices become part of every aspect of life, issues of responsible use, privacy, and security will inevitably follow.

Reshaping Institutions

Focus Questions

1. How are mobile devices changing the way people work, and are these changes beneficial? Explain your answer.
2. Should there be rules for the use of mobile devices in the classroom? Why or why not?
3. Should there be restrictions on how apps use personal information? If so, what might they include and why? If not, why not?

"Every now and then a truly disruptive technology appears and causes major changes in business, society, and economies. . . . Mobile computing is this type of disruptive technology."

— Michael Saylor, entrepreneur, founder, and CEO of MicroStrategy, Inc.

Michael Saylor, *The Mobile Wave: How Mobile Intelligence Will Change Everything*. Boston: Da Capo, 2012.

Mobile devices are not just changing how people communicate, seek information, or shop. These devices are also offering opportunities and posing challenges to social institutions, government, and business. Mobile devices have had an effect on journalism, for instance. Mobile devices are being used to capture local events and stories that would have been largely invisible to traditional media outlets. However, when combined with photo-sharing services, mobile devices make it easy to capture and spread images that are misleading, inflammatory, or used for propaganda purposes. Political campaigns, too, have been forced to come to terms with the instant exposure possible through mobile devices. An ill-considered statement will be seen by millions within just a few hours.

In this new media environment the risk of being misinformed has grown. Many people now rely on their mobile device as their primary source of news, and many apps make it easy to select only news sources that agree with one's existing views. This can limit the opportunity to encounter other viewpoints or more factually accurate sources.

Many other institutions and activities are being reshaped by access to this technology. Mobile devices are reshaping how teachers teach, students learn, doctors treat illness, and patients look after their own health. Increasingly, these developments are not limited to the advanced industrial nations of North America and Europe or the growing economies of Asia. In less developed parts of Africa and Latin America mobile devices are helping nations essentially skip building the wired communications systems of the twentieth century and move directly to the wireless twenty-first. Michael Saylor believes:

> Developing nations are leapfrogging into the twenty-first century with the help of smartphones and tablets and cell towers. I firmly believe this will be a game-changer for the global economy: the ability to deliver a First World education—as well as critical, time-sensitive information—to nearly everyone. . . . By 2015 . . . we're going to have 4.5 billion such devices connecting people worldwide. Mobile communications can only improve the quality of life for most, particularly in those parts of the world where paved roads and crowded airports are things left to the imagination.[25]

Mobilizing Change

Along with social media, mobile devices are an increasingly important part of modern political campaigns. By 2014, according to a Pew Internet survey, 28 percent of registered American voters

What Services and Information Do People Access by Smartphone?

Mobile devices are changing many areas of modern life. According to a 2015 Pew Research Center report, a significant percentage of the US population uses smartphones to obtain information about health and for online banking. Many also use their smartphones for house hunting, job searches, and more.

Percent of Smartphone Owners Who Have Used Their Phone to Do the Following in the Last Year

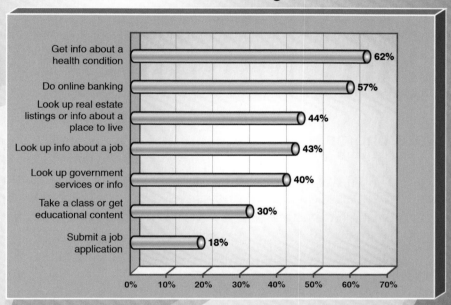

Source: Pew Research Center, "More than Half of Smartphone Owners Have Used Their Phone to Get Health Information or Do Online Banking," Internet & American Life Project, March 31, 2015. www.pewinternet.org.

were using their cell phone to follow political and campaign news. This is twice the percentage observed only two years earlier.

With people increasingly using mobile devices rather than print media or even home Internet as their main news source, those working on campaigns know they cannot ignore the mobile audience and its preferred means of communication. E-mails sent out from campaigns may be overlooked, particularly by young people who consider e-mail to be rather old-fashioned. Even Facebook may be too detailed to navigate for people who want something short and to the point. Twitter, with its stream of short messages linked by topical hashtags, attracts people by its immediacy. When, for example, protests broke out in late 2014 over deaths of unarmed black people at the hands of police in Ferguson, Missouri, and New York City, Twitter streams, along with live video, made the events seem immediate.

Two aspects of Twitter amplify its potential power for campaigns. One is the choice of a hashtag that is so memorable that it becomes a symbol of a movement. After terrorists kidnapped 276 female students from a Nigerian school in April 2014, activists were frustrated by the lack of government response. After about a week the hashtag #BringBackOurGirls had appeared in about 2.3 million tweets thanks to Twitter's "retweet" feature that makes it easy to forward any message to all of a person's followers.

Watching or Helping?

Sometimes the choice to use one's mobile device for social good is closer to home. The mobile world is often viewed as a self-centered one. (The fad for taking "selfie" photos in every conceivable location has been offered as an example.) Yet the mobile world can also mobilize compassion and cooperation.

The choice of taking a picture or taking action came to one witness on January 28, 2015, when a devastating fire destroyed an apartment house in San Francisco's Mission District. As residents, many weeping, fled the building leaving most of their possessions behind, blogger Zach Crockett was dismayed by something else he saw: bystanders who calmly held up their smartphones to make videos of the disaster but showed little inclination to help the victims. In this age where videos go viral and spread effortlessly even as people watch them passively, Crockett realized, "I could really only think of one thing as I watched your building burn: that inside each apartment families were raised, meals were shared, memories were made. I didn't want to just be passive."[26]

Crockett decided he wanted to do something to actually help the victims of the fire. He started a page on GoFundMe, one of many crowdfunding sites that can be used to gather contributions for a project or cause. He thought he might raise as much as $2,000. In just a few days, however, schools held bake sales, churches collected donations, and 2,300 people and businesses (including Google) made donations. The $165,606 obtained was turned into a check for between $6,000 and $15,000 for each family or individual that had been made homeless by the fire.

> **crowdfunding**
>
> Funding a project or venture by raising money in small amounts from many people, usually over the Internet.

Taking Control of Health

Another aspect of modern life that is being reshaped by mobile devices is health care. Health is everyone's concern, and the vast health care industry is a major part of the economy. The growing cost of health care has been driven in considerable part by the more complicated health needs of an aging population and the potentially lifesaving but expensive new devices used to diagnose and treat diseases. However, technology in the form of mobile devices and accessories may offer lower-cost alternatives while giving people more control over their health information.

Activity or fitness trackers have already become popular, especially for people who want to monitor their running, walking, and other exercise. These devices can be clipped to clothing or worn as a wristband or as part of a smartwatch. They measure distance traveled (including altitude change) and heart rate. The devices often send their data to a linked smartphone. However, a growing number of smartphones have built-in activity trackers. Apple's HealthKit app lets users view a dashboard that tracks data such as blood pressure, blood sugar and cholesterol, exercise, weight, and calories burned. Looking to the future, Hal Varian, chief economist for Google, suggests in a Pew Center report that "you will be able to purchase health-monitoring systems just like you purchase home-security systems. Indeed, the home-security system will include health monitoring as a matter of course. Robotic and remote surgery will become commonplace."[27]

Fitness trackers (pictured) are popular with people who want to monitor their running, walking, and other exercise. Some of these devices can be linked to a user's smartphone.

Mobile devices can also bring medical services to people in remote areas where there may be no clinics. Developed by researchers at the University of California at Berkeley, the Cell Scope attaches to a smartphone's camera and turns it into a microscope. A person with minimal training can slide in a blood sample and the Cell Scope can tell if the patient has malaria or tuberculosis. If so, the image can be sent to a medical professional for further analysis.

Mobile and wearable devices can be used for medical research as well as diagnosis. For patients with complex conditions such as Parkinson's disease, it is hard to gauge how symptoms may be progressing or monitor the effectiveness of treatment based only on brief doctor visits. A joint project of Intel Corporation and the Michael J. Fox Foundation (MJFF) is using the accelerometers built into smartwatches to make detailed records of the patients' gait and tremors. The readings are then subjected to sophisticated analysis. According to MJFF CEO Todd Sherer,

accelerometer

An instrument that measures changes in speed or direction.

"Our hope is that the use of these technologies can help develop a therapy to slow or stop Parkinson's progression."[28]

Other devices can help manage chronic diseases. Diabetes, for example, requires careful and continual management of a patient's blood sugar level. With LifeScan, developed by the pharmaceutical company Johnson & Johnson, a small glucose monitor is attached to an iPhone. Following a simple finger prick, the monitor uploads its reading to an app that can estimate how much insulin will be needed and when, taking into account the patient's diet and meal schedule. The app will then alert the patient when it is time for an insulin injection.

Managing a Flood of Innovation

While these and other new devices and apps offer exciting possibilities for improving health care, two challenges must be faced. One is regulatory. These devices and many related apps are subject to regulation by the federal Food and Drug Administration (FDA). This regulatory process can be complicated, time-consuming, and expensive. App developers and mobile innovators, on the other hand, are used to a fast pace from development to market. Striking a regulatory balance that ensures devices are safe while allowing for their rapid development may not be easy.

The other challenge is how the flood of detailed medical information gathered by these new devices can be managed by patients and doctors so that it actually results in better health or treatment decisions. As health care blogger John Lynn notes: "Once the patients collect all this data, how are doctors going to use that data, and how can they digest this wave of information that will come from these devices? I don't think we know that yet."[29]

Meanwhile, although doctors are increasingly taking advantage of electronic medical records, coordinating care has still meant phone calls, answering services, or voice mail and delays that could be critical during emergencies. Sunny Tara, an iPhone app developer, believes that "in this day and age, with on-demand real-time information, that's uncalled for."[30] Tara's app, DocBeat, lets doctors communicate directly with each other, keeping their schedules up to date so, for example, an emergency department doctor knows which specialists needed for a particular critical case are available. Other apps provide interactive checklists that doctors can use to make sure they do not miss a step in examining a patient or evaluating findings to make a diagnosis. Before writing a prescription the doctor can use the Epocrates app to consult an up-to-date database on possible dangerous interactions with drugs the patient is already taking.

Reshaping Education

Like health care, education is a vast enterprise that involves a variety of professionals. And like doctors and patients, teachers and students are finding both opportunities and challenges in how mobile devices affect their work. For example, when Katie Denton, a North Carolina high school junior, has trouble with algebra, she can get help right away. Her school has provided every student in her class with a smartphone as part of a pilot program called Project K-Nect. At first, Denton explains, "I was trying to figure out how a phone was going to help me with math."[31] Denton then learned that she could use her phone to send messages to her teacher or a fellow student, asking for help with a math problem. She can watch a video that demonstrates math concepts. She can even post to a blog where students can discuss their struggles with and ideas about math.

Assessments showed that students in the algebra classes in K-Nect who used smartphones outperformed those in regular classes taught by the same teachers. The students used their phones at least an hour a day to do their homework, and overall, they spent significantly more time working on algebra.

Besides helping students with traditional academic subjects such as math, teachers and students are finding ways to use smartphones to extend learning into new areas. Because the built-

Mobile Devices in Schools:
Positives and Negatives

Educators seem to be divided about whether mobile, Internet-enabled students are gaining or losing educationally. According to a 2014 survey by the Pew Research Center:

> 77 percent of teachers say the Internet and digital search tools have had a "mostly positive" impact on the students' research work. [But at the same time] 87 percent agree these technologies are creating an "easily distracted generation with short attention span."

> 76 percent of the teachers strongly agree "the Internet enables students to access a wider range of resources than would otherwise be available." [However] 76 percent strongly agree that Internet "search engines have conditioned students to expect to be able to find information quickly and easily."

> 65 percent agree to some extent that "the Internet makes today's students more self-sufficient researchers" [but] 83 percent agree that the "amount of information available online today is overwhelming to most students."

> 90 percent agree that "the Internet encourages learning by connecting students to resources about topics of interest to them." [but] 71 percent agree that the digital technologies "discourage students from using a wide range of sources when conducting research."

Lee Rainie, "13 Things to Know About Teens and Technology," Pew Research Center, July 23, 2014. www.pewinternet.org.

in camera makes it easy to shoot photos and videos, for example, some teachers are having students interview World War II veterans about their wartime experiences and record photos or videos of the interview. These can then be added to their reports or presentations. Mapping and GPS software can be used to survey local wetlands for a class in environmental science. If students working together on a project discover they need more information about a topic, they can find it online right away and then continue their work. Throughout the semester students can use apps designed to help them set up a class schedule, manage their time, and communicate with each other and their teachers.

Finding a Balance

Although new technologies can empower teachers and learners, they have also posed the challenge of how to integrate them into the classroom. When personal computers first became widely available in the 1990s educators and schools struggled to find appropriate ways to use them in the classroom. At first the cost of the machines and the lack of teachers trained in their use often limited computers to special computer labs that students would visit for perhaps one period a day. Many of today's students, however, have grown up in a world where Internet access is an everyday given. Further, as writers Cathie Norris and Elliott Soloway observe, "Even for K–2 youth, [the] smartphone is fast becoming a must-have, not a nice-to-have. From providing entertainment to supporting communications, from providing personal security to supporting social interactions, K–12 students will be equipping themselves, during 2015–2020 with smartphones—especially when they can be purchased for less than a pair of trendy tennis shoes!"[32]

If students have ready access to their devices throughout the school day, there is the danger that they will be more absorbed in their phones than attentive to what is being taught. In response, one editorial opinion in 2010 seemed to favor simply banning the distracting devices. "Cellphones may be conduits for information, but they're also tools of mass distraction. Texting, tweeting, surfing and updating your online profile have nothing to do with learning and no place in the classroom. Yet it's even become commonplace for parents to text their children during school hours. What are they thinking?"[33]

What really seems to be needed is a way for teachers and students to agree on when to use their devices and when to set them aside to avoid distraction. Writer Toni Fuhrman suggests, "One of the most successful is *not* to ask students to put their phones away, but simply to leave them visible on their desks. This discourages students from holding the devices on their laps while they text and tweet away. Indeed, classroom instructors might want to take a page from the airlines, asking students to power off their electronic devices for the duration of the flight."[34]

Rather than just restricting their use, some educators suggest a more positive approach. They believe that students who bring mobile technology to school should be gently guided to the best uses of their devices. Ed Lyell, a business and education professor who has observed the growth of the Internet over decades, believes:

> Just-in-time learning will continue to expand, permitting people of all ages to find the information they need when needed. It will permit the human mind to focus on creativity and critical thinking with known information being available as needed. Time in school will need to radically change since the talking-head, expert teacher is less and less valuable. The role of teacher-coach will be even more important yet require a different emotional and intellectual skill set than that which most educators now possess.[35]

Opportunities and Disruptions

The use of mobile devices is having a major impact on many professions and industries. While the specific details and issues differ, these impacts have something in common: They are disruptive to existing institutions. This can be seen most clearly by looking at how different types of business are being affected. In business, a disruptive innovation changes the way markets are structured and how consumers behave. The result is that existing business models begin to fail, while innovators who can adapt to the new reality can sometimes achieve rapid success.

The first wave of disruption in modern times was based on the widespread use of the Web. Amazon became hugely successful, first in selling books and eventually in selling virtually anything else that can be shipped. By taking advantage of its size and efficient

The explosion of online businesses such as Amazon (the company's distribution center in Phoenix, Arizona, is pictured) became a disruptive force for traditional brick-and-mortar stores. Widespread use of mobile devices is having a similar effect on many types of businesses.

software Amazon has been able to dominate the market and force publishers to offer it favorable terms. Physical brick-and-mortar bookstores and other stores have found it hard to compete with Amazon's rock-bottom prices and fast shipping.

Mobile devices represent the latest wave of disruption. By 2014 more than 20 percent of American consumers were using mobile devices as their primary access to the Internet—and this number is expected to increase. Not being tied to a physical location, mobile users increasingly expect to be able to connect to any service, from anywhere, and at any time of day.

This has several implications for businesses, starting with how people find them. Instead of typing into a search engine such as

Google at a desktop or laptop, mobile users increasingly use voice-based searches. When confronted with a leaking toilet, the user might take out a phone and say something like, "OK, Google, where can I find a good plumber?" Apps such as Google Now or Siri are (or soon will be) smart enough to know that the user wants someone in their neighborhood, and of course will know from the phone's GPS where the user is located. To determine who might be a "good" plumber, the search app can use ratings services such as Yelp.

The increasing use of mobile apps and rating services means that restaurants (and service businesses such as plumbers) have to pay close attention to how they are rated on Yelp and other social media. A plumber wants a high rating on Angie's List, a popular ratings site for service businesses. Someone who has just arrived in a city and needs a last-minute hotel booking might look for reviews on TripAdvisor. That same traveler might find a restaurant that sounds good and use OpenTable to get a reservation. Thus mobile devices add to the already great importance of the online world even for traditional brick-and-mortar businesses such as restaurants and shops. In just about any store selling appliances, electronics, or furniture, customers are going to be looking at merchandise, taking a picture (or scanning a bar code) with their phone, and using an app to get price comparisons from Amazon and other online retailers.

The Sharing Economy

The new mobility is also blurring the line between businesses and consumers. For example, people can run a small business from home by selling goods on eBay or can self-publish and sell a book on Amazon or another service. Now mobile devices take this a step further by allowing people to become part of the "sharing economy" in which people provide resources directly to other people for a fee. A person can drive his or her own car for Uber or Lyft and take paying passengers who are connected to the service by a mobile app. Airbnb lets a person rent out his or her room or whole apartment, and apps make it possible for travelers to quickly find a place to stay. Regulators who are used to dealing with traditional taxicabs or hotels are now scrambling to come up with rules for these new services.

Cheaper and Easier but Also Disruptive

Mobil device apps have made it easier and cheaper to get a ride, but these apps have also disrupted businesses that have traditionally provided this service. With services such as Uber and Lyft, users directly connect to a driver and car through a mobile device and often are picked up within a few minutes. The fee for such service is often less than what would be paid for the same ride in a taxicab.

Many passengers find these services to be faster and more convenient than traditional taxis, which are often in short supply. As attorney Brandie Mask notes, "In a city like Houston where you can't get a cab on the street (or very quickly from a call most of the time) it is life changing to have cheap car service available within minutes. Also, it's great to have the same service in different cities so you don't need to figure out the cab situation in an unfamiliar place. You just open your trusty app."

However, while cabs are tightly regulated with regard to fares and operating conditions, regulators were caught flat-footed by the rapid growth of the new networks. In 2013 California's Public Utilities Commission issued regulations that require driver background checks, insurance, and special licensing for drivers who take part in ride-sharing services. However, some cities declared the new services to be illegal and ordered them to be shut down.

Quoted in Denver Nicks, "Like It or Not, Uber Is Transforming Life in Middle America," *Time*, December 9, 2014. http://time.com.

The trend toward paid "sharing" may have gone too far with an app called MonkeyParking. This app lets someone getting ready to leave their parking space "sell" the space to the next waiting car for a fee. However, parking spaces belong to the public. San Francisco city attorney Dennis Herrera sent a cease-and-desist letter to the app's developer stating that it was creating "a predatory private market for public parking spaces that San Franciscans will not tolerate."[36] MonkeyParking's makers fired back, arguing on free speech grounds: "I have the right to tell people if I am about to leave a parking spot, and they have the right to pay me for such information."[37]

Whether in professions such as health care or education, or in the numerous businesses people deal with every day, the emergence of disruptive applications of mobile devices shows no sign of slowing down. Even as consumers are offered more choice and entrepreneurs seek new opportunities, the effects on social and economic life will continue to raise troubling issues.

The Future
of Mobility

Focus Questions

1. How might the widespread use of wearable devices affect privacy and social expectations?
2. What are some benefits and risks of developing the Internet of Things?
3. How do you think people will be using mobile devices in 2020?

"The growing number of connected devices, especially mobile ones, is progressively changing the way people perceive, experience, and interact with products and each other."

— Michal Levin, senior user experience designer at Google.

Michal Levin, *Designing Multi-Device Experiences: An Ecosystem Approach to User Experience Across Devices.* Sebastapol, CA: O'Reilly Media, 2014, p. 3.

The capabilities of mobile devices and even the forms they take will continue to surprise. However, some trends may provide clues to the mobile devices of 2020 and beyond. Physically, the devices will continue to become more powerful and capable, rivaling many desktop computers. When combined with the increased connection speeds offered by the service providers, the streaming of music, videos, and even games, already popular, is likely to become virtually continuous. Displays will continue to increase in resolution and will incorporate forms of 3-D viewing.

Not only will mobile devices become more capable, but they will also change in size, shape, and how they are used. Wearable devices such as smartwatches from Apple and other companies and head-mounted devices such as Google Glass represent only the first generation of what is likely to be the next stage in mobile evolution.

What Are the Possibilities?

More powerful and versatile mobile devices will change the way people interact with one another and with everything in their environment. A 2014 Pew Research Center article suggests that a number of killer apps—ones that virtually everyone will use—will emerge in what Pew researchers call the Gigabit Age. The Gigabit Age refers to a time when broadband access speed is at least a billion bits per second—and it is already dawning in a few pioneering communities. The ability to move large amounts of data at high speed will make new applications possible, even routine.

Already many people use Skype, Apple's FaceTime, or other similar services to have meetings or interviews in which the participants can see and hear each other. At present poor connections or slow, choppy video is not uncommon. But with more widespread high speed mobile service, coupled with the convenience of mobile devices, Pew's experts suggest that

telepresence

The ability to see and interact with people and objects in a remote area without being physically there.

"people's basic interactions and their ability to 'be together' and collaborate will change in the age of vivid telepresence—enabling people to instantly 'meet face-to-face' in cyberspace with no travel necessary."[38]

Besides connecting people in ways that seem more like face-to-face encounters, mobile devices will also help people connect to the information they need to manage daily life in an increasingly complex world. Other experts surveyed by Pew thus suggest, "The connection between humans and technology will tighten as machines gather, assess, and display real-time personalized information in an 'always-on' environment. This integration will affect many

A bridesmaid who was unable to be at her best friend's wedding in Colorado was able to participate through an iPad and FaceTime. Apps and other online services allow people to interact without being in the same place.

activities—including thinking, the documentation of life events ('life-logging'), and coordination of daily schedules."[39]

To see more specifically where mobile technology might be heading, it is useful to look at some new kinds of devices that are already coming on the market. As one might expect with the early versions of a new technology, these devices come with limitations and questions about their utility and appropriate use.

Smartwatches: Useful Tool or Fashion Accessory?

Before there were smartphones, the mobile device that most people wore was a wristwatch. Digital watches, which used electronics rather than springs or motors to keep time, first appeared in the 1970s. In the 1980s and 1990s some computer features (such as a calculator or a simple text display) began to be added to digital watches. In the early 2000s several watches ran computer operating systems, but their tiny screen gave them little value as stand-alone computing devices.

It became clear to developers that the main utility of smart-watches would be as an extension of the smartphone. The Pebble Smartwatch, released in 2013, can display incoming calls, e-mail, and social media notifications from a connected smartphone. The watch can also be used to control phone functions, such as making calls or taking pictures.

In early 2015 Apple released the Apple Watch. This device takes advantage of thorough integration with Apple's iPhone and can run a variety of apps. Apple's watch is expensive (starting at $350, up to $10,000 or more for a fancy gold version) and stylish. However, it is not clear whether it or its competitors will be widely adopted. People are already carrying a computer in their pocket—their smart-phone. Does the convenience of not having to pull it out to check for e-mail or make a call outweigh having to buy a second device? (Ironically, many people in recent years stopped wearing traditional watches because they could check the time on their smartphone.) Perhaps, like fancy traditional watches, the smartwatch may be mainly bought as a status symbol or fashion accessory. This does not necessarily mean the devices will not be successful. As one analyst notes, "Apple's Watch is perceived as something that is aes-thetically desirable rather than something that is technically interest-ing, and there is a far higher demand for the former."[40]

Glasses That See Everything

If smartwatches do too little to become must-have devices, head-mounted mobile devices such as Google Glass may do too much to be comfortable for many people to use in daily life situations. Nevertheless, this first genera-tion of head-mounted devices has found some interesting uses. In 2013 Google offered the result of years of research into head-mounted computers. Mounted into the corner of a pair of eyeglasses,

early adopter

Someone eager to try out new technologies.

Google Glass was offered to early adopters—people who like to try out new technology ahead of the general public—at a price of $1,500. Google Glass displays information directly in the user's

Tracking in the Workplace

Mobile devices can empower people, but they may also be used to monitor them. Chris Brauer, a professor at the Institute of Management at the University of London, suggests to employers, "These devices can tell you under what conditions your workforce is most productive, under which conditions your workforce is most alert and what makes them happier and more satisfied in their jobs."

Brauer studied the use of three devices: a wristband that measures movement, a headset to monitor brain activity, and a wrist strap that monitors posture and reminds the wearer to sit up straight. He suggests that employers could experiment with these devices and determine which employees "are not functioning optimally." Working conditions might be changed to help such employees, or they could be replaced by "other employees who are better conditioned for your environment." Brauer suggests that employees will be happier if studies like this redirected them into more suitable jobs.

Brauer acknowledges that while having employees who are better suited to their work might give a business a great competitive advantage, it might be difficult to get employees' consent to participate in such studies. There are of course privacy issues whenever an employer collects or stores information about employees. However, even given both consent and privacy protections, in an economy where the bargaining power of most workers has been declining and job choices may be few, there is the specter of workers having to choose between accepting such monitoring or becoming unemployed.

Quoted in Bloomberg BNA, *HRfocus*, July 2014, p. 1.

field of vision. A tiny touch pad can be used to control the device and select from among events such as phone calls, photos, and social network updates. The device can also be given commands such as, "OK, Glass, take video!" A variety of applications were available, including ones such as Google Maps, Foursquare, and OpenTable, frequently used by travelers. A companion smartphone app makes it easier to set up the glasses and specify preferences.

Joshua Topolsky, a technology journalist who tried Google Glass, found he appreciated that he could view alerts for phone calls or text messages without having to constantly pull his phone out of his pocket. He found the device to be particularly useful when traveling. Any directions he needed while walking in an unfamiliar city could be popped up right in the corner of his vision. "In the city, Glass makes you feel more powerful, better equipped, and definitely less diverted," Topolsky notes. He observes that "[Glass] brought something new into view (both literally and figuratively) that has tremendous value and potential. . . . The more I used Glass the more it made sense to me; the more I wanted it."[41]

Other people who tried Glass, such as Boston University media studies director James Katz, were less enthusiastic. Says Katz, "I found that it was not very useful for very much, and it tended to disturb people around me that I have this thing."[42] The built-in camera allows the user to take pictures or video at any time. Some movie theaters banned the devices, fearing they were being used to make copies of movies. In other places such as bars and restaurants, Glass users have sometimes been verbally (and in a few cases physically) assaulted. The pricey gadgets may also arouse anger from people who believe they have been displaced by a new class of rich techies.

As with smartphones being used during meetings, social situations, or in public, it may take some time to get to some sort of agreement on what is socially acceptable. An anonymous user commented to Google staff, "It may be that new social norms develop with Glass, where people develop an informal way of showing they're not using it—say, wearing it around their neck to signal they aren't using it or being distracted by it."[43]

Perhaps in response to its mixed reception, in early 2015 Google announced that it had halted sales of the early version of Glass, saying that future versions were in development. Historically, Google has shown that it has the resources and willingness to try, fail, and then try something different. Meanwhile, other companies are bringing out their own versions of eyeglass computers. Sony, for example, introduced in 2015 a SmartEyeGlass Attach device that can help runners and pedestrians navigate. It can be easily clipped onto or removed from one's eyeglasses. The success of this kind of technology and the forms it may eventually take remains an interesting question.

Augmented Reality

In addition to displaying navigation helps or reminders, eyeglass computers offer the possibility of letting people see information about any object they might be looking at. This application is called augmented reality. While augmented reality apps are somewhat useful on smartphones, they come into their own as part of wearable devices such as Google Glass and Microsoft's HoloLens. The latter not only puts information into the user's visual field, but it also tracks the user's head position so it knows where a person is looking and responds to gestures and voice commands. For example, if someone is interested in learning more about a painting in an art gallery or an artifact in a museum, he or she just looks at it and can see a relevant article from Wikipedia. On a hike, one can see a bird and instantly find out its species. As a more practical, everyday matter, looking at a sign for a business or other building could bring up information about who is there and when they are open.

augmented reality

The display of relevant information about objects in the environment.

The applications for augmented reality in daily work seem limitless. A worker in a warehouse driving a forklift would not have to consult a printed map or even a smartphone app to find out how to get to the next stack of pallets. The most efficient route, complete with turns, simply appears in the corner of his or her eyeglasses. A soldier on patrol could see the exact position of enemies hidden by night and fog. A driver would be alerted to an approaching obstacle—perhaps a lane blocked by an accident.

Augmented reality may make many jobs easier and safer, but it can also make new ways of working possible. Instead of having to look repeatedly at an X-ray or a screen, surgeons could see through the body even as they make an incision. Rather than having to look up information in a database or make tedious calcula-

A demonstration of Microsoft's HoloLens shows how the new wearable device technology can be used to test and develop robotics. Experts say this and other augmented reality devices have potential for many areas of business and daily life.

tions, researchers could visualize genes or molecules in whatever degree of detail is required and manipulate them in a 3-D virtual environment.

In general, as the Pew report suggests, "Augmented reality will extend people's sense and understanding of their real-life surroundings and virtual reality will make some spaces, such as gaming worlds and other simulated environments, even more compelling places to hang out."[44]

However, even as new devices make augmented reality part of daily life, the issues already raised by earlier mobile devices will continue to be raised. Augmented reality offers useful information, but inserting it into the user's field of vision has the potential to be quite distracting. Even privacy is affected: In order to show relevant information about what someone is seeing, the device needs to "know" where people are and what they are doing. That stream of user information, like that generated by browsing the Web or using mobile apps, can be mined for targeted advertising—including, perhaps, ads projected right into the field of vision.

Mobility and the Internet of Things

Mobile devices already allow users to connect to people and places in new ways. However, they will soon allow users to control a wide variety of devices, at home and out in the world. The idea of a remote control is not new—it goes back decades to the device that enables one to change TV channels without physically touching the TV. More recent are modules that one can install to remotely control lighting, heating, air-conditioning, and other devices around the home. However, now that just about every significant device has a computer built in, the potential for having devices automatically send and receive information and commands is being increasingly exploited to create what has been called the "Internet of Things."

Traditionally, a home or office building's lighting, security system, and heating, ventilation, and air-conditioning (HVAC) systems would be purchased separately. They would have no connection to each other. However, if the devices include the ability to communicate in a standard way, many new efficiencies and capabilities become possible. These include monitoring energy use in a building or environmental conditions such as air or water quality outside. People who are willing to install smart utility meters, lightbulbs, furnaces, and so on may receive discounts on their utility bills because the utility will be able to automatically reduce energy use during peak times or emergencies. Meanwhile Internet providers such as Comcast and AT&T have entered the home security market. In 2014 Google acquired Nest, a manufacturer of devices

The Brain as Mobile Device

Mobile devices have changed how people communicate, obtain information, and see their world. Wearable devices may accelerate this process of change because of their accessibility and close connection to the body. But what if the brain itself could connect to a mobile device that could help one remember things? In a series of experiments, researchers led by Sam Deadwyler of Wake Forest University demonstrated that the memory of how to do a task could be recorded electronically from the brain of a rat, erased (using a drug), and then reloaded so the rat again remembered what to do.

Although much work would be needed to create a reliable system for recording and replaying human memories, a person with dementia might be able to record memories and retrieve them later when needed. As USC professor of engineering and lead study author Theodore W. Berger notes, "If you're caring for someone in the house, for example, it might be enough to keep the person out of the nursing home."

What about transferring new information from a computer directly to the brain? This would require understanding much more about exactly how brains take in, organize, and store information. But someday a device implanted in the brain may make today's smartphones and tablets obsolete. However, the idea of one's thoughts being spied upon or even manipulated by hackers would be enough to frighten even the most avid technology enthusiasts.

Quoted in Benedict Carey, "Memory Implant Gives Rats Sharper Recollection," *New York Times*, June 17, 2011. www.nytimes.com.

for "smart homes." They and others will offer increasingly comprehensive packages that combine data/media, home control, and security functions.

Mobile devices such as phones or tablets are ideal for remotely controlling or monitoring all these integrated systems. An app running on the mobile device would provide a dashboard that shows basic information (such as temperature and energy use). By touching a few menus the user can get more detailed information, such as a profile of energy use for the past month. Smoke and CO_2 sensors could send warnings directly to the mobile device. Break-ins or other security breaches would not only send alarms but also live video from security cameras. An important added benefit is that the user does not even have to be at home to monitor and control all those smart devices.

The Internet of Things extends beyond the home. Other mobile apps could enhance existing navigation capabilities by providing real-time traffic and road conditions picked up from a network of sensors. From there it is only a step further to have the app use this real-time information to find a faster alternate route. In stores, communications-enabled packaging and shelves might communicate directly with the shopper's mobile device, touting special prices and deals. Integration with mobile payment systems such as those from Apple and Google would greatly speed up checkout. These possibilities lead many industry analysts such as Peter Middleton of Gartner, Inc., to be enthusiastic about the growth of the Internet of Things:

> By 2020, connectivity will be a standard feature, even for processors costing less than $1. This opens up the possibility of connecting just about anything, from the very simple to the very complex, to offer remote control, monitoring and sensing. As product designers dream up ways to exploit the inherent connectivity that will be offered in intelligent products, we expect the variety of devices offered to explode.[45]

A New World of Mobile Devices

However, this new world of mobile devices connected to just about everything adds to the already widespread concerns about security and privacy. Rogue apps or malicious hackers could attack the mobile device and obtain information about a security system, including access codes. Alternatively, the connected devices could be attacked and either sabotaged or used as vectors to implant viruses or other malware. Even if security is not directly compromised, apps could use the information that will become available about someone's energy use or living habits to add to the flood of targeted advertising. An article by the American Civil Liberties Union (ACLU) warns:

There's simply no way to forecast how these immense powers—disproportionately accumulating in the hands of corporations seeking financial advantage and governments craving ever more control—will be used. Chances are Big Data and the Internet of Things will make it harder for us to control our own lives, as we grow increasingly transparent to powerful corporations and government institutions that are becoming more opaque to us.[46]

Since the devices will come from different manufacturers, it will be hard to regulate the many possible configurations of these systems. Some combination of regulation of apps and devices and development of industry standards seems to have the best chance of managing the Internet of Things. At a February 2015 US Senate hearing, Adam Thierer, a senior researcher at George

An electric toothbrush connected to a tablet could provide the user with information about his or her brushing practices. This is just one small example of what is possible as the Internet of Things develops and expands.

Mason University, suggested that regulators take a cautious approach to regulating the emerging Internet of Things: "We got policy right with the 1990s. . . . Now we need to get it right for the IoT. We need a light-touch, market-driven approach without trying to anticipate problems."[47]

However, in a report on its 2013 workshop *The Internet of Things: Privacy & Security in a Connected World*, the Federal Trade Commission (FTC) expresses serious concerns that the Internet of Things, by vastly increasing the possible connections and the amount of data flowing, may make existing security and privacy problems considerably worse. Many of the recommendations they make are similar to those already given for mobile apps. However, since the Internet of Things involves the design of hardware as well as software, the FTC says, "Companies should build security into their devices at the outset, rather than as an afterthought. As part of the security by design process, companies should consider: (1) conducting a privacy or security risk assessment; (2) minimizing the data they collect and retain; and (3) testing their security measures before launching their products."[48]

Beyond Mobile Devices

People who encountered the Internet in the 1990s will remember the phrase "Web surfing." This meant sitting down at a computer, looking at favorite websites, and following interesting links. However, Dries Buytaert, founder of the Drupal Web platform, believes that the Web is essentially being turned inside out—from something people visit to something people essentially live within:

> The current Web is "pull-based," meaning we visit websites or download mobile applications. The future of the Web is "push-based," meaning the Web will be coming to us. In the next 10 years, we will witness a transformation from a pull-based Web to a push-based Web. When this "Big Reverse" is complete, the Web will disappear into the background much like our electricity or water supply.[49]

"Push" means that apps are constantly displaying messages and notifications on mobile devices. It will no longer be necessary to remember to "check for mail" or look to see what's on the day's schedule. The user will be reminded of that and many other things. As Buytaert suggests, that will mean the Web will no longer be a separate place that one goes to find things. Similarly, the connections to the Cloud and the Internet of Things will mean less focus on devices—even mobile devices—and more on the content being displayed. Ultimately, with everything connected to everything and information flowing in continuous streams, the mobile device as people think of it today may seem as quaint as the floppy disk–driven desktop personal computers of the 1980s.

Introduction: The Anywhere, Anytime World

1. Richard Stengel, editorial, *Time*, August 27, 2012, p. 4.
2. Rich Ling, *Taken for Grantedness: The Embedding of Mobile Communication into Society.* Cambridge: MIT Press, 2012, p. 24.
3. Ling, *Taken for Grantedness*, p. vii.

Chapter One: How Did the World Become Mobile?

4. Quoted in Mike Cellzik, "Buried in Haiti Rubble, U.S. Dad Wrote Goodbyes," *Today*, January 19, 2010. www.today.com.
5. Arthur C. Clarke, interview, AT&T/MIT Conference, 1976. www.youtube.com.
6. Quoted in Brian X. Chen, *Always On: How the iPhone Unlocked the Anything-Anytime-Anywhere Future—and Locked Us In*. Boston: Da Capo, 2012, p. 9.
7. Chen, *Always On*, p. 122.
8. Mark Mulligan, "How the App Economy Has Transformed Product Strategy," *Music Industry Blog*, October 11, 2012. https://musicindustryblog.wordpress.com.
9. Quoted in Gerry Smith, "Smartphones Bring Hope, Frustration as Substitute for Computers," *Huff Post* Tech, June 6, 2012. www.huffingtonpost.com.

Chapter Two: Mobile Devices and Daily Life

10. Michael Saylor, *The Mobile Wave: How Mobile Intelligence Will Change Everything*. Boston: Da Capo, 2012. Kindle edition.
11. Saylor, *The Mobile Wave*.
12. Joe Colton, "Smartphones, the Most Pervasive Interruption Technology Ever," *FilterJoe* (blog), May 6, 2011. www.filterjoe.com.
13. Colton, "Smartphones, the Most Pervasive Interruption Technology Ever."
14. Quoted in Brian X. Chen, "Help! My Smartphone Is Making Me Dumb—or Maybe Not," *Wired*, October 4, 2010. www.wired.com.

15. Quoted in Chen, "Help! My Smartphone Is Making Me Dumb—or Maybe Not."
16. Quoted in Chen, "Help! My Smartphone Is Making Me Dumb—or Maybe Not."
17. Quoted in Matt Richtel, *A Deadly Wandering: A Tale of Tragedy and Redemption in the Age of Attention*. New York: William Morrow, 2014. Kindle edition.
18. Quoted in Kathiann Kowalski, "Watch Out: Cell Phones Can Be Addictive," *Science News for Students*, September 20, 2014. p. 1.
19. Susan Davis, "Addicted to Your Smartphone? Here's What to Do," WebMD. www.webmd.com.
20. Hewlett-Packard Corporation, *Mobile Application Security Study 2013 Report*. www8.hp.com.
21. Kamala Harris, California Attorney General, *Privacy on the Go: Recommendations for the Mobile Ecosystem*, January 2013. http://oag.ca.gov.
22. John Brownlee, "This Creepy App Isn't Just Stalking Women Without Their Knowledge, It's a Wake-Up Call About Facebook Privacy," Cult of Mac, March 30, 2012. www.cultofmac .com.
23. Federal Trade Commission, "FTC Report Raises Privacy Questions About Mobile Applications for Children," February 16, 2012. www.ftc.gov.
24. United States Supreme Court, slip opinion, *Riley v. California*, 2014.

Chapter Three: Reshaping Institutions

25. Michael Saylor, *The Mobile Wave*.
26. Quoted in Kevin Fagan, "Blogger Hands Out $165,000 to Mission Fire Victims," *San Francisco Chronicle*, February 26, 2015. www.sfchronicle.com.
27. Quoted in Lee Rainie, Janna Anderson, and Jennifer Connolly, *Killer Apps in the Gigabit Age*, Pew Research Center, October 9, 2014. www.pewinternet.org.
28. Quoted in Jane McCallion, "How Wearable Devices Could Save Your Life," *PC Pro*, January 2015, pp. 124–25.

29. Quoted Caitlin McCarry, "Docs Go Digital: Nudged by Federal Mandate, Health Care Takes Steps Toward Electronic Future," *Las Vegas Business Press*, March 12, 2012, pp. 7–8.

30. Quoted in McCarry, "Docs Go Digital."

31. Quoted in Michelle R. Davis, "Solving Algebra on Smartphones," *Education Week*, March 18, 2010, pp. 20–23. www.edweek.org.

32. Cathie Norris and Elliott Soloway, "The Holy Grail of Educational Technology Is Within Sight," *TheJournal*, October 27, 2014. http://thejournal.com.

33. *Maclean's*, "Don't Give Students More Tools of Mass Distraction: Texting, Tweeting, and Surfing Have Nothing to Do with Learning and No Place in the Classroom," September 29, 2010. www.macleans.ca.

34. Toni Fuhrman, "Virtual Personal Assistant App Helps Students Manage College Life," *Campus Technology*, January 12, 2015.

35. Quoted in Rainie, Anderson, and Connolly, *Killer Apps in the Gigabit Age*.

36. Quoted in Brad Tuttle, "Can We Stop Pretending the Sharing Economy Is All About Sharing?," *Money*, June 30, 2014. http://time.com.

37. Quoted in Tuttle, "Can We Stop Pretending the Sharing Economy Is All About Sharing?"

Chapter Four: The Future of Mobility

38. Rainie, Anderson, and Connolly, *Killer Apps in the Gigabit Age*.

39. Rainie, Anderson, and Connolly, *Killer Apps in the Gigabit Age*.

40. Quoted in Benny Evangelista, "Pressure on Apple to Prove New Watch Is Worth the Cost," *SF Gate*, March 9, 2015. www.sfgate.com.

41. Quoted in Charles Arthur, "Google Glass: Is It a Threat to Our Privacy?," *Guardian*, March 6, 2013. www.theguardian.com.

42. Quoted in Arthur, "Google Glass: Is It a Threat to Our Privacy?"

43. Quoted in Rachel Metz, "Google Glass Is Dead; Long Live Smart Glasses," *Technology Review*, November 26, 2014. www.technologyreview.com.

44. Rainie, Anderson, and Connolly, *Killer Apps in the Gigabit Age*.

45. Quoted in Ian Parker, "The Shape of Things to Come," *New Yorker*, February 23, 2015. www.newyorker.com.

46. Quoted in Preeti Gaur, "Impact of the Internet of Things," *PCQuest*, October 2014, pp. 24–25.

47. Quoted in Jedidiah Bracy, "Senate Committee Explores Internet-of-Things Regulation," Privacy Advisor, February 12, 2015. https://privacyassociation.org.

48. FTC Staff Report, *Internet of Things: Privacy & Security in a Connected World*, January 2015. www.ftc.gov.

49. Quoted in Matt Asay, "The Future of Mobile May Not Look Like Apps," *Readwrite*, March 13, 2015. http://readwrite.com.

Books

Brian X. Chen, *Always On: How the iPhone Unlocked the Anything-Anytime-Anywhere Future—and Locked Us In.* Boston: Da Capo, 2012.

Roman Espejo, *Smartphones.* Detroit: Greenhaven, 2013.

Harry Henderson, *The Digital Age.* San Diego, CA: ReferencePoint, 2012.

Michael Saylor, *The Mobile Wave: How Mobile Intelligence Will Change Everything.* Boston: Da Capo, 2012.

James P. Steyer, *Talking Back to Facebook: The Common Sense Guide to Raising Kids in the Digital Age.* New York: Simon & Schuster, 2012.

Internet Sources

Distracted Driving Facts and Statistics. www.distraction.gov/get-the-facts/facts-and-statistics.html.

Mary Madden et al., "Parents, Teens, and Online Privacy," Pew Research Center, November 20, 2012. www.pewinternet.org/2012/11/20/parents-teens-and-online-privacy.

Pew Research Center, "Mobile Technology Fact Sheet." www.pewinternet.org/fact-sheets/mobile-technology-fact-sheet.

Casey Phillips, "How Smartphones Revolutionized Society in Less than a Decade," Government Technology, November 20, 2014. www.govtech.com/products/How-Smartphones-Revolutionized-Society-in-Less-than-a-Decade.html.

Privacy Rights Clearinghouse, "Fact Sheet 2b: Privacy in the Age of the Smartphone." www.privacyrights.org/smartphone-cell percent20phone-privacy.

Aaron Smith, "Pew Research Findings on Politics and Advocacy in the Social Media Era," Pew Research Center, July 29, 2014. www.pewinternet.org/files/2014/07/PAC-Aaron-Smith-Presentation.pdf.

Eric J. Topol, "The Future of Medicine Is in Your Smartphone," *Wall Street Journal*, January 9, 2015. www.wsj.com/articles/the -future-of-medicine-is-in-your-smartphone-1420828632.

Websites

C/Net: Mobile Latest News (www.cnet.com/topics/mobile). Includes news and reviews of mobile devices, hardware, and apps.

***TheJournal:* Being Mobile Blog** (http://thejournal.com/being mobile). Reflections and news about the use of mobile devices in education.

Mobile Phones News (www.techradar.com/us/news/phone -and-communications/mobile-phones). Latest news about mobile devices and operating systems.

***PC Magazine:* Mobile Apps** (www.pcmag.com/reviews/mo bile-apps). Reviews and offers top one hundred lists of the best apps for iPhone, iPad, Android, and Windows Phone.